PURPLE ADOBE

By

Christopher J. Helvey

ISBN: 0-7596-9875-9 (E-book)
ISBN: 0-7596-9876-7 (Paperback)
ISBN: 0-7596-9877-5 (Dust Jacket)

This book is printed on acid free paper.

1stBooks - rev. 03/13/03

DEDICATION

This work is for
O.J. and Marjorie W. Helvey
My Parents
Who made everything possible

CHAPTER 1

The day died a purple death against the cracked adobe walls.

Twilight rose like a nocturnal tide, crested the splintered window sill, and lapped across the dust covered floor. I lay in a dark corner with my back against the cool adobe, knees curled up against my chest, head heavy on my arms, and watched the purple waves of evening devour the final golden slivers of the day.

The air in the room was still and hot, holding on to the fierce heat of the day. Dust motes danced in final light of day and I watched, with one brown eye closed, their final pirouettes of death. It seemed as if I could taste them deep in my throat. They were coated with a message for me, but I couldn't decipher it.

I had a notion that if I lay very still, for a very long time, that somehow, perhaps through osmosis, the meaning that they held might filter through the lining of my throat and float languidly up to my brain. Why these messages, born in the wild and carried by the desert winds, were important wasn't clear to me. At least, not yet. Still, I knew that they were important. I lay inert on the smooth polished stones that formed the crudely squared floor of the hacienda and stared transfixed at the dying light until a purple darkness covered me.

A cactus wren sang a clear lullaby, but I didn't sleep. I lay as still as the stones beneath me and watched a silvery coin rise from the undulating floor of the desert that fanned out in all directions from my lonely adobe. The minutes piled up like shiny new quarters on the floor beside me. A full moon peered in through my cudely curtained window and shone full into my single open eye. The moonlight was cool and fluid and bore deep into my soul. There was no mercy, no kind caress, only truth's cool shaft of penetration.

1

CHAPTER 2

They came with the morning sun. I saw the three of them as they crested the long, undulating hill that rose behind my adobe keep like some medieval castle. My side of the hill was the western side and as such got the bulk of what little rain passed this way. My castle grounds weren't carpeted with lush green grass, but here and there sparse patches of dull green sprouted and tall scraggly horse weeds forced their way through the rocks that littered the hillside like fallen soldiers.

Tiny at first, they grew larger as they came down the steep slope. For the first five minutes I couldn't tell if they were little men, women, or wizened old gnomes. Only when they had closed to within fifty yards of my place could I see that they were children. Thirteen or fourteen years old I guessed. Indian. At least they had some Indian blood flowing through their veins. Navajo I guessed, although I wasn't the best judge of tribal traits. Still, it was a good guess. When I got this place from old Josh Baxter he had told me that the reservation extended to within a half mile of the eastern slope of the mountain that formed the fortress behind my back door. He noted in passing that sometimes a tribal member crossed over the border but that it was rare and they had never given him a moment's trouble.

I hadn't been here more than two months and these were the first inhabitants of the reservation who had come onto my land. Perhaps they didn't even know I existed. Baxter had said that they would speak when spoken to but never made any efforts to initiate conversation. That suited me just fine.

The sun was at their backs and their shadows grew elongated and spread across the dusty brown ground like three pools of dark liquid poured from a giant's cup. They were still twenty yards away from the house when their shadows brushed against my adobe.

Their hair was black and shiny in the morning sun. It hung long down their backs and swayed gently as they angled down the hill toward me. Occasionally the morning breeze lifted a strand and flapped it like the broken wing of a young vulture.

I had heard that long hair was the style among the young men on the reservation, and I had assumed that the three young bodies traveling single file along the narrow track that wound torturously like a coiled serpent through the rocks, sand, and scraggly cactus were all male. It wasn't until they were within ten yards of the hut that I could see that I was wrong.

The short, thin, wiry looking one in front was a girl. Small breasts that poked at her thin shirt like pointed pebbles were a dead giveaway. Her eyes were dark and sunk deep in her head, but she was lighter in coloring than the other two. I could tell now that her hair was more brown or maybe even chestnut than black, and there was a different angle to her cheekbones. More Anglo blood flowed through her veins.

The other two were more pureblood. Hair black as jet and obsidian eyes that gave away nothing. The middle one was short, squatty, and looked older than the girl. Not that he was ancient, but she didn't look over sixteen to me. He had a sour look on his face as if he had just tasted over-aged milk. The trailer of the trio was taller, thinner, and walked with a limp. His left leg was bothering him, and his hair hung down in his face so that often I could only see one eye at a time. I wondered how he could see where he was going.

A stronger breeze sprang up and swung around the corner of the house. It whipped in through the open window and the tattered blue sheets I was using as curtains fluttered in response. The trio stopped in their tracks and stood like stone statues on the hill side. For a long moment they were silent as the sands of the desert that ran before them like the flat shallows of a long lost inland sea. Then the girl turned and I could hear murmurs, too faint for me to discern any words. Once, when the wind paused for breath, I thought I could hear something about "somebody living there now", but then my imagination tended to run wild in the dry air that hovered above the desert.

Board meeting over, the two males slipped away from in front of my window and quickly moved to encircle the hut, moving in opposite directions more quietly than they had come down the hill. The girl squatted on her heels and stared straight ahead. A thought wandered momentarily across the inside of my mind that she could see through the adobe and then through me to the empty blackness that hid my heart. I felt naked and exposed, as if I were stretched naked on an operating table and she were poised above me, scalpel in hand. I gritted my teeth and cursed myself for a coward.

As if she could read my mind, she rose from her heels and began to walk very slowly, but with an immense certainty about her, toward the adobe. Little puffs of dust danced at her heels. She was close enough now so that I could see the freckles that dusted her cheeks and the gold flecks that swam in her brown eyes, spaced too far apart in her small, fine skull.

I couldn't hear the footsteps any more at the sides of the house. The morning breeze sighed deeply and drifted off to find the cool shade of the cottonwoods that grew along the little creek that trickled at the far end of the long valley which spread to the west. Hot air migrated in through the glassless windows and brought the promise of another scorcher. The sun had completely crested the hill now and blazed away as if it were intent on baking my adobe again.

The girl was within five yards of my window now. I could count the hairs on her long eyelashes and see the beads of sweat form across her upper lip. Golden flecks danced in eyes the color of old walnut furniture. Her lips were full and stretched across a mouth that was too big for her face. I knew I was in full shadow behind my cool adobe walls, but I still had the uneasy, certain sense that she could see me; see more of me than I could see myself. I am not often afraid, but this slight teenager with the overbite frightened me. With her wonderfully strange eyes, she was a seer; a seer of souls. My soul was not ready for a public display, and I wished her gone from my life forever. She knew too much and I had so little. It wasn't fair that she should steal the secrets from my soul.

Soul-reading slut. She smiled—slyly, shyly—and allowed me to see the spaces between her teeth. She needed braces, a bath, and a beautician, and I had nothing to give. I bared my teeth in the dark. Her dark vision was great and she saw and chuckled deep in her throat at my false bravado, putting her mark on my soul. Then she cried a strange high cry that I couldn't understand, turned and ran up the hill, back the way she had come. The other two cut the angle and joined her halfway to the top. At the crest they ran on, but she turned and extended one arm toward me in a gesture that I could not comprehend. She paused there, silhouetted against the glory of the morning for just a moment. But her image burned in the back of my mind for days.

CHAPTER 3

She came on the third day after the visit from the unholy trio. The mid-morning sun shone brightly against her face, and she had to squint until her eyes were blue BB's to see well enough to pick her way up the winding rock strewn path that climbed the hill like an ancient snake, made fat and slow with the relentless passage of time. The reflection off her Jeep Cherokee parked in the arroyo below was blinding. I watched her make thirty yards in a minute and a half before I turned from the glassless window and went and lay on the narrow wooden bunk rammed up against the west wall of the best room. As an afterthought, I pulled my Tijuana blanket up tight under my chin. It wasn't a suit of armor, but then I wasn't a knight of the Round Table.

It took her two more minutes to make it to my door. I could hear her blowing hard like a winded mare, and I rolled over and pressed my unshaven face against the cool adobe wall.

Her knock was firm against the flimsy door. It seemed to dry rot more each day, and I could hear it shudder in its frame like the death rattle of an old prospector. I lay as still as the silent sands of the desert. Her feet shuffled restlessly on the gravel-pocked sand that lay in small mounds before my door. I closed my lips tightly and pretended that I was a single weathered stone in the wall of the great canyon.

"Mr. Evans?" The door swung open as though in response to her voice. The hinges were rusty and groaned in protest. Her voice was a trifle nasal and a half-pitch high. It grated on my nerves. I shut my eyes and thought about a grove of cottonwoods I had once seen along the Rio Grande.

"Mr. Evans, are you awake?"

The voice was softer and lower now but still nasal. I thought about the cool brown waters of the Rio Grande and let the silence between us lengthen. I wasn't ready yet. Wasn't ready for the world to come intruding on my solitude, that peaceful healing that only undisturbed silence can bring.

She was inside now. I could hear her feet shuffle across the earthen floor. A bold bitch, I thought to myself, to come uninvited to a man's house and then when he didn't answer the door to just come on in anyway. I was tempted to do several things, but I didn't want trouble, a confrontation, or even a conversation. I wanted my peaceful solitude, the undisturbed sanctity of my own private seclusion. I really just wanted to be left the hell alone, by everybody. I wasn't being discriminatory.

Her breath came in soft little puffs as she stood by my bed. I was suddenly conscious of the fact that I hadn't bathed in I couldn't remember when. Too damn bad for her. If I were lucky, she was the sensitive, pristine type.

She cleared her throat, trying to swallow away some of the dust. Maybe she would choke. "Mr. Evans, I have come one hell of a long hot way and I am not going to leave until you and I have a conversation. So, you might as well turn over so we can have our little chat."

Inwardly groaning, I rolled over so that I was on my side facing her and cracked open one eye about half a slit. "Sorry to disappoint you, but I ain't Mr. Evans." My voice sounded strange in my ears. Then I realized that I hadn't spoken in better than a week. Little wonder my vocal chords felt strange.

"Yes you are." She sounded petulant, mad at me for not cooperating and half-pissed at the rest of the world because she was hot and tired and I was being a discouraging prick.

I went right on being one. "No, I'm not."

"Yes, you are." Doubt had begun to seep into her voice.

"How do you know?"

Logical enough question, but it gave her pause. "They told me so."

"Who told you so?"

"Those men. The men down in the valley. The men at Jenkin's store."

"Do you know them?"

She frowned at me and ran a wet tongue across sandpaper lips. "No, but they seemed like honest people. They told me Ward Evans bought the old Baxter place, and you are Ward Evans. Aren't you?"

She waited for me to respond, and the silence fell between us like a thick velvet curtain. Through my half closed eyes I watched the dust motes dance in the dry desert air.

"I know this is the old Baxter place. They gave me specific directions. They were easy to follow; I know I didn't mess up." More confident now, sure of her directions and her ground.

"Maybe they lied to you."

A slender hand brushed at dust that had possessed the audacity to settle on her cheekbones. They were good cheekbones, well-formed and set high in a heart shaped face. Clear green eyes stared at me from under long lashes. She was forty, give or take, but a well preserved forty. Man's plaid shirt tied at the waist and jeans that strained to contain the apple firm cheeks.

Aerobics, jogging, and free weights three times a week; all the American male wanted and more. Also less. Not my style. I shut my eyes. Too much light, too soon.

"They didn't lie," she said fiercely. I wondered if the fierceness was there to convince me or herself.

I gave her half a smile. I hadn't brushed my teeth in a week. They had to be dusty yellow. My breath was sour in my own mouth. I hoped she had enough sense to stay the hell away from me. "This might be the Baxter place, but like I told you before, Evans I am not."

"Yes you are!" She stamped her foot prettily and a little puff of dust rose up and settled on her handmade calfskin boots. "You look just like your picture, the one in the *Times*, well, except for that undergrowth on your face. Mr. Evans, this is not *Miami Vice* and you are not Don Johnson." She half-smirked at her own cleverness.

"No, it's not *Miami Vice*, and I am not Ward Evans." Tiring of the inanity of the conversation I rolled over and sat up. I was careful to keep my back against the wall and my lower body covered up. I wanted her to leave, not see my raggedy Hanes.

"But you are," she spluttered in protest. "I know you are. Just because you deny it doesn't make it not be true. Life just doesn't work that way. You can't simply run away from who you are."

"Lady, don't try to tell me about life, especially my own. This is America and I can be whomever I want to be, whenever I want to be. Just for the sake of ending this insanity, let's say at one time that I used to be this Ward Evans you're rattling on about. The point is that at this moment in this time and space I am not Ward Evans and won't be, no matter how hard you want me to be."

I could hear a tint of rising anger coloring my voice and that only served to make me all the madder. I didn't like this woman being here. I liked it even less that she could arouse any emotion in me, even anger. I had come to the desert for its healing solicitude, its great void of emotion. I wanted no part of mankind and the unhealthy aura of emotions that surrounded the species.

Her too clear green eyes stared at me. I could almost hear the inner workings of her brain. She stood silently for a long moment before she made her decision. Then she crossed the small room and did a backwards straddle on one of the two rickety wooden ladder backed chairs that were serving time with the weathered oak table. She wrapped both arms on the top rung and rested her small round chin on her soft, tanned flesh.

"Maybe it'd work better if I introduced myself first and told you why I'm here. My name is Gloria Gibson and I want you to help me find my daughter." There was a smile on her lips that died halfway to her eyes.

7

I told myself to shut the fuck up. "She missing on purpose?" I never seem to take my own good advice.

"That I don't know, Mr.——. You know, it would help if I had a name for you? What are you calling yourself these days?"

"I've been called lots of names. You can use Sanchez."

"First or last name?"

"Doesn't matter. You only need one. Use it or get lost."

Gloria Gibson sighed deeply as if I had offended her. "All right, Sanchez. I'll play your silly game. I need help. I'm told that when you want to be, you are the best man in the world at finding someone, whether they want to be found or not. My only daughter dropped off the face of the earth just over six weeks ago. No one knows where she went or why, or at least that's what they're telling me. Melissa and I may not have always had the perfect mother and daughter relationship, but we always stayed in touch. She always called me whenever she needed money or a shoulder to cry on, and she needed one or the other or both at least every couple of weeks. Therefore, I need you. I want my daughter found and I want her found quickly."

She paused for breath, and I interjected, "What if she doesn't want to be found?"

"What do you mean, if she doesn't want to be found?"

"There are times, Ms. Gibson, when some people, especially young girls, don't want to be found by anyone, especially not by their parents. How old is Melissa?"

She choked the disbelief back down her slender throat and faintly murmured, "Nineteen."

"That's old enough to get lost and stay that way if she wants to. Not a lot that you can do about it." I was looking out the open window, but I could hear the pain in Ms. Gibson's moan. I ignored it. "You did notify the police?"

"Yes. They let me file a missing persons report, but they were about as insensitive as you. They told me that, at her age, Melissa could basically come and go as she pleased. I was left with the distinct impression that they would file the report and do just enough to cover their official behinds and that would be the end of their efforts." Her sigh was dramatic and full of disgust. "The only help I got was when a sergeant gave me your name."

"Who was that?"

"I believe his name was Nichols."

"Santa Fe?"

"Yes. Is something wrong?"

She had heard more in my voice than I had intended. "Something is always wrong in this world. Now go away and leave me alone."

"But what about Melissa? Will you help me?" The plaintive whine in her voice was disgusting.

"I'll think about it. Leave your name, address, and phone number on the table. If I decide to look, I'll be in touch. Oh, and if you have a picture of Melissa, leave it too." I closed my eyes and lay back on the bed.

I could hear her take one halting step toward me, and I sensed that she wanted to tell me more, touch me in some way, but she came no closer. In a moment I heard the rustle of some paper, then some time later the jeep engine coughed. I lay quite still and listened to her bump and grind her way back to the valley. When I could hear the engine no more, I got up and went outside. I sat for a long time under a white hot sun.

CHAPTER 4

I put the snapshot in my shirt pocket and opened the car door. Melissa Gibson's picture wasn't that easy to forget. Her broad brow and deep purple eyes framed by palomino blonde hair stayed with me all the way up the long white sidewalk. At the end of the concrete was a long low-slung ranch of pinkish brick and oversized white sculptured shutters. Had to be at least five bedrooms. I was willing to bet my next check that a significant part of the backyard was an in-ground pool.

The doorbell was deeply inset and surrounded by gold filigree. The whole effect made me want to look at my hands to be sure my fingernails were clean before I pressed the buzzer. I pressed the buzzer anyway, without looking.

In a moment I caught the echo of footsteps. The hallway must have been a long one because the steps seemed to come on forever. Then, suddenly, the door was flung open and a bikinied Gloria Gibson stared back at me. She was quick, but not quite quick enough to out-smile the ripple of surprise that rose rapidly in her eyes. Droplets of water stood on her hard, tanned hide. In ten more years she would turn into leather. I wondered if she was as hard inside as out.

"So, you did come after all." Her marble hard green eyes worked their way over my face and drifted down south. "You clean up nice too."

"You must have either inherited or married your money."

The sly smile faded from her face. "What do you mean?"

"You're too damn dumb to have earned your money the honest way. When are you going to learn that flattering me, or attempting to, is a waste of your time? In fact, it works against you."

Ice was starting to form on the green pools, but she kept a note of civility in her voice. "I am sorry, Mr. Sanchez. I assumed that since you had come to see me you had decided to look for Melissa. I was only trying to be friendly."

"Don't be. I don't have the faintest desire to be your friend. However, I have decided to help you look for your daughter, if we can agree on terms."

She dabbed at some stray droplets that had gathered just above her eyebrows. Her blonde head inclined toward the rear of the house. "Come on out back and we'll talk." She swiveled quickly on limber hips, and I followed her twitching muscular legs down exactly the long cool hall I had imagined.

Gloria paraded across the pebbly walkway that surrounded the oval pool and flopped down on a webbed beach chair patriotically striped in red, white, and blue. "Mr. Sanchez, I meant what I said the other day about needing your help. I still need it. I am not an independently wealthy woman, but I do have some money. Name your terms, and if there is any way possible, I will meet them." Tiny beads of sweat had popped out on her upper lip and she licked at them with the point of her moist pink tongue. There was something feline in the gesture.

"My needs are simple. You give me a full answer to every question I ask, pay me two hundred a day and expenses, and I do it my way. If I find her, I'll talk with her. If she wants to come home I'll bring her. If not, I'll let you know."

Her eyes were now hidden behind one hundred and twenty-five dollars a pair Oakleys, so I watched her Adam's apple go down and up in her elegant neck. "Those are harsh terms, Mr. Sanchez." She paused before she gave me a smile that barely brushed her lips. "However, I don't have a lot of choice in the matter. I want my daughter found, and I am told by people I trust that you are the man to find her." She licked her lips again. "How much do you want as a retainer?"

"Eight hundred."

She rose slowly from the beach chair, letting me see the length of her legs and the slimness of her arms. "I'll go get my checkbook."

I cursed myself for a fool as my eyes followed her across the deck. I hoped Melissa was worth giving up my private purple adobe.

CHAPTER 5

Santa Fe, oh my Santa Fe; the homecoming queen has grown tired of fighting the battle. Overrun by the never ending hordes of tourists, she has sold herself to the highest bidder. She will lift her skirts for any tourist bearing the almighty dollar, but beneath her rhinestones and mascara there are still traces of her true beauty.

I pulled inside the high russet adobe walls that surrounded the Pueblo de Bandas. As always, dozens of red and yellow ribbons hung from the twisted branches of the withered old mesquite tree that still struggled in the front left corner of the nearly square courtyard. I pulled my six year old Cherokee to a stop before the split rail fence that fronted the office, turned off the ignition, and watched the dust settle on the faded green hood.

A tiny yellow bird swayed back and forth on the thick black wire that ran from the greasy black utility pole to the small bungalow that functioned as the office. Business must not have been too good lately. There were unpatched holes in the screen, and the wooden door and window frames hadn't seen a coat of paint in several summers. I walked across the gravel with stiff joints and a dull ache in the small of my back. The yellow bird twittered at me from his high perch. It sounded suspiciously like laughter.

The screen door squeaked on its hinges as it swung open. I let it close with a sharp wooden clap. Dust motes rose up and floated through the late afternoon sunlight that spilled from a long four-paned window to greet me. It was quiet enough in the hot little room to hear my own breathing. A long-faced cow's skull, hung on the wall as a memento mori, stared down at me from its vacant eye sockets. Though it was long dead and bleached as white as the snow on the top of the Jimenez Mountains, it gave me the willies. A nervous sweat ran down the middle of my spine. I shrugged my shoulders to ward off the spirit and walked with purpose to the counter. Scores of knife scars and inked expressions of lack of imagination and intelligence blended into a counter-top mosaic. I smacked the top of the brass bell.

A small child with a runny nose poked his head around the door frame. He gave me a long look through great brown eyes. I must not have impressed him as being extraordinary fierce because he wobbled on into the room on unsteady legs dragging a rather ragged teddy bear by one dirty, tattered hind leg. He tottered across the floor and stood staring up at me. He gurgled several words that I couldn't begin to understand then blew a bubble at me.

"Silva, come here." The authoritative voice belonged to a decidedly unauthoritative body. She was tall and slender with a big hooked nose and thin, muddy brown slits for eyes set between pock-marked cheeks. She was dark, and of mixed ancestry. Her thick lips looked incongruous in her thin skull. They reminded me of the big orange paraffin lips I used to buy as a kid at Halloween.

"Señor, I am sorry," she said between the thick lips. "Can I help you?"

"John around?"

"Who?" Confusion muddied her voice as well as her eyes.

"John Morris, the man who owns this place. Is he here?"

"Oh, sí, Mr. Morris. No, he is here no longer. Juan and I, we bought this place from him a year ago in March. I am sorry, I did not know his first name. My husband handled most of the business. My husband and the banker, John Ross. You want I should get him for you."

"Mr. Ross?"

"No, Juan. You understand? My husband."

I understood all right, but I didn't like what I was hearing. I was tired of the conversation though, and the woman, and, at least for the moment, living. I nodded my affirmation.

I heard her go away, small quick steps that sounded sharply on the wooden floor. The child was still in the room and I could hear it sucking and sniffling. I kept my eyes closed. It was easier that way. My imagination was bad, but not as bad as reality. I leaned against the counter and thought about John. I wondered where he was, what had happened to him. We had crossed mountains and forded streams together. We had shared beans and coffee and once, the same woman. My friends were few and far between these days, and I could ill afford to lose another one.

"You wished to see me, Señor?"

I opened my eyes. He was about two inches shorter and ten years younger than I was. His waist was thick, but the cords of muscle in his forearms strained against the rolled up fabric of his plaid workshirt. There was a small, white scar just to the left of his mouth, and intelligence danced in his brown eyes.

"I'm looking for John Morris."

"He is no longer here. My wife and I bought the place from him last year."

"Do you know where he is?"

"No, I am sorry. He only stayed in town for a few weeks after he sold this place to me." He shrugged his shoulders.

"Why'd he sell out?"

"Señor, you seem to know him better than I do, perhaps you could say." He put a crooked grin on his smooth brown face.

"Was he traveling alone or with someone?" I could hear the frustration in my own voice. I hadn't seen John in a couple of years and had been looking forward to renewing our friendship. Besides, John was a man who kept one ear close to the ground. In the back of my mind I had been counting on him as a source of gossip to give me a lead or two on Melissa.

"The last time I saw him he was in the company of a lady."

"Young?"

A shrug. "Not so young, not so old. Maybe thirty, thirty-five."

"Blonde?" John had always favored golden hair.

"No, her hair was black. Her money though was green, very green. She opened her purse once," he answered in response to my unspoken question, "and I could see it. She had a great deal of it. Enough, as the vaqueros say, to choke a horse. I only saw her twice. I am sorry, but I do not know where Mr. Morris or his young filly went. She was a lively stepper though, that much I can say."

Bully for John, I thought. "You still rent rooms by the night?"

"By the day, the week, the month, your pleasure. I have three rooms available right now. Would you like one?"

"Number fourteen was always lucky for me." It was also the only room that backed onto Carson Circle, a little loop of a street that enabled you to take either of the main drags out of town or go straight downtown without everyone in the Pueblo de Bandas knowing your business. I was a very private person.

Juan smiled broadly, showing me a full set of large, white teeth. "Your luck is still good. Number fourteen is one of the three that are not occupied. Only twenty dollars a night, or one hundred and twenty-five if you take it for a full week." He gave me that big grin again.

"One week," I promised Juan, Gloria Gibson, and myself.

CHAPTER 6

The old man sat with his head drooping on the bench outside the Silver Cactus. Twin saddlebags hung low under his eyes. His scraggly whiskers told me that he hadn't shaved in a week. He smelled like he hadn't taken a bath in two. As my shadow fell across him, he stuck his chicken leg of an arm at me. A white Styrofoam cup half full of loose change was at the business end.

"Help a disabled veteran, buddy?"

I shook my head and closed my nose against his stench, brushing by him. I resisted the urge to tell him to get a grip on himself. My guess was that whiskey, not combat, was his problem. Getting off the sauce, taking a shower, and running a razor across his stubble would push him a long way down the road to stability.

The Silver Cactus was just another fancy name fronting for a tourist trap. It was a Southwestern version of a French bistro. You could get a semi-edible sandwich and a double priced drink from a faux-cowgirl who showed you all of her teeth when she took your money. It was the sixth place I had hit today, and I didn't figure on staying long. The Silver Cactus was barely a third full.

The bar was horseshoe shaped and the color of cow dung. The bartender looked like Walter Brennan on steroids. I sat down on a cracked leather stool and ordered a Bud Lite. He brought me an icy mug and gave me his second best smile.

"That'll be two dollars."

With prices like that, Gloria Gibson's expense money was going to mount up in a hurry. I slid a five and the snapshot of Melissa across the counter in his general direction. "I know you recognize Abe, how about the girl?"

He took a long look down his short, flat nose then started to shake his head from side to side. I caught a glimpse of the dawn of recognition in his eyes just before he stopped his denial. Thick fingers gently plucked the photograph from the dark countertop. He twirled the picture so that it picked up more of the little light that existed inside the Silver Cactus and screwed up his eyes as if they were binoculars that he was adjusting. The hair on the back of his hands was thick and matted like an animal's.

"I couldn't swear to it, the light ain't so good in here, but it favors a girl that was coming in here for a while."

"She's not coming now?" I could feel the excitement that had begun to bubble up inside me start to subside.

"Not lately." He rolled his little piggy eyes. "I'd say that she hasn't been here for the better part of a week. Course I don't work all the time, so she could have changed her schedule and started coming in when I was off."

"Was she drinking a lot?"

The bartender tried to refresh his memory by gnawing on his thick lower lip with what were surprisingly small, even, white teeth. He wanted me to know how hard I was making him work for his lousy three dollars. "Can't say that she was. Most nights she usually nursed a margarita. Course, once or twice, when somebody else was buying, she let herself go a bit. Got downright polluted one night."

"You catch her name?"

He shook his cannonball of a head ponderously. "Sorry, man. She might have told me, but I never paid much attention. They come and go so fast in here. I only know my real regulars."

He must have read the disappointment in my eyes. "Hey man, don't panic. There's this dude comes in every day about this time that she sat with several times. I'll bet he can help you." A smile spread slowly across his muscled face.

"You know his name?"

"Sure. It's Mike, Mike Brown. Like I told you, mister, I know all my real regulars."

He handed me the picture as if he were sorry to see it pass from his hands. I understood. Melissa was lovely in the right light.

"You wouldn't be her daddy, would you?" His concern sounded genuine.

"No, but her mother hired me to look for her. Can you tell me what this Mike Brown looks like?"

His smile broadened. He liked to be of service. "I can do better than that. He just came in, sitting at the round table in the far left corner. See him? With the redhead. Tall, slim fellow with the shaggy silver hair."

I nodded and slid him another picture of a dead president.

*　　*　　*

"Yeah, I've seen her. Had a drink or two with her as a matter of fact. Paid for them, too, if that's important." He laughed a little, either to himself

16

or at himself, I couldn't tell which. "You a policeman?" His smile of welcome was still on his face, but there was a faint line of wariness around his eyes.

"Strictly private. Just trying to help a mother find her daughter. You get to know Melissa well?"

He shook his shaggy silver head from side to side. He was forty trying to look thirty trying to look forty. The line of jaw was still youthful and he held his slim body erect. His eyes, however, had seen a lot of life and they were old, an aged, faded blue. "We never got on the same wave length. So, Melissa is her real name." He chuckled. "She was calling herself Sage when she was here. I knew that wasn't likely to be real, but what the hell. We all want to be somebody else from time to time. I don't see much harm in changing your name."

"Me either. What did you two talk about?"

Brown flashed a quick look at the redhead before he answered. Even though she was sitting down, I could tell that she was tall. Her jawline was strong, and her green eyes were nearly hidden by thick mascara and spider leg eyelashes. She gave Brown a look I couldn't decipher. He shrugged his shoulders.

"We talked about a lot but said very little, if you know what I mean. Sage, I mean Melissa, was a tough person to get to know. We never really did connect. Chemistry just wasn't there." He smiled sheepishly at the redhead. "Not that I tried all that hard anyway."

"Wouldn't she talk?"

"Not much. Oh, she might comment on the weather, or some silly television show that had been on recently, but as far as in-depth conversations, we didn't have much. Course, she was drinking a lot, and some people are just quiet drinkers. The only subject she was really hep on was this dude she was trying to find."

"Who was he?" I could feel the excitement beginning to bubble again. I tried to keep it out of my voice. You could never tell how it would affect someone. Some responded to it, others completely clamed up at the first sign.

Brown didn't seem to notice. "Seems like she told me, but I can't for the life of me think of it right now." Brown swallowed about half of the amber contents of his glass and gave me a friendly smile. "I do remember his picture though."

"Melissa had a photograph of this man?"

"Yeah, she showed it to me every time she got really plastered, which was two, maybe three times."

"What'd he look like?"

My voice must have sounded harsher than I intended. Brown winced a bit, and the redhead turned her spotlights on me. "Well, let's see. He was a guy in a light colored suit, striped tie, head full of dark hair."

"You've got a good memory," I said in a more gentle tone. "How old would you say?"

"Thirty, maybe thirty-five. Kind of hard to say. The picture wasn't that good."

"Did it look like a new snapshot?"

"No, it had been handled quite a bit before I saw it. One of the corners was bent, and it had a big crease right down the middle."

"Thought of the name yet?"

Brown shook his handsome head. "Sorry. My old brain's tired tonight." He took another drink and put his free hand over one of the redhead's. Her fingers were very long and slender, with what had to be three inch nails. "You might try over at the Inn of the Governors. I think I heard her say once she was staying there."

"Thanks." I rose slowly, but had the feeling that I was missing something. If I was, it wouldn't come to me. "If you think of the name to go with the photo, you can contact me at the Pueblo de Bandas. Ask for Sanchez."

"Sure. Nice to meet you." The look the redhead gave me said she didn't agree. I wondered what I had done to piss her off. Maybe nothing in particular. Sometimes I just have that effect on people, especially women.

The old man snored gently on the bench outside. His styrofoam cup had picked up a little change and a single one dollar bill. He looked very peaceful in the twilight, almost young under the dirt and stubble. I wondered if his mother knew, or if she cared.

CHAPTER 7

Their silver lay before them like the treasures that had led Cortez across thousands of miles of sand and sagebrush, up ragged, rugged mountains, down into infernos masquerading as valleys. Silver had brought a few wealth, a few poverty, a few insanity. But ultimately, what it had brought was death. Not just to brave men, beautiful women, and innocent children, but death to a way of life, an entire civilization.

There were twenty or so this evening, their bracelets, necklaces, and pendants arranged before them on brightly colored, hand-woven blankets spread on the sidewalk that ran for a long block across the street from one side of the little park that formed the heart of the downtown square of Santa Fe. They were relatively few in number tonight. The tourists would outnumber them twenty to one before the night was over, and they seemed strangely conscious of this fact.

Huddled together under the wooden awning that ran the length of this block, they sat with their bronze backs to the wall and stared out at the rest of Santa Fe with ebony eyes so deep that you could see for centuries and never get to the bottom.

I resisted the urge to go and sit with them for an eternity, instead cutting across the grassy park on my way to the Inn of the Governors. Like them, I was different; a man lost in his own time and space. Yet I didn't belong to them either. I wished I was back in my little crumbling adobe, watching another day die a purple death wrapped in a shroud of gold.

*   *   *

"Yes, I've seen her." The eyes of the girl behind the counter were sharp and black in her brown face. I could almost hear her sharp mind clicking into gear. She closed her lips together firmly as her dark eyes dared me to try and get her to say more.

"Recently?"

"Why do you want to know?"

"Her mother hired me to look for her."

"For real?" Surprise in the voice, and ten years off the face. I liked her better this way. The real person was some nice young *mestizo,* almost young enough to be my daughter.

I gave her my safe-to-be-with and easy-to-believe smile. "For real. Her mother hired me yesterday. I drove down to Santa Fe last evening. I don't know what she told you, but her real name's Melissa Gibson. She's old enough to be on her own, but maybe not mature enough to know how to handle it, if you know what I mean. Growing up is hard for some people. They either don't do it or they get it wrong. As a matter of fact, I haven't quite got it right myself."

The girl bent her head down and studied the ledger book in front of her with unseeing eyes. "She told me her mother was dead." She raised her head slowly and stared into my eyes. Her eyes had gone suddenly liquid. She swallowed hard and I watched her Adam's apple bob up and down. Uncomfortable, I looked away from her face. The badge on her white silk blouse was red with gold trim. The black letters of her name read Maria.

"I believed her, too," she said half in anger. Sadness was the other half. "She stayed here for the better part of a month. We had lunch together almost every day. I thought we were friends." Her sadness was partly for herself. I understood; friends are few and far between.

"How long ago did she leave?"

Maria dabbed at her eyes with a Kleenex. "Five or six days, maybe a week. I don't know. She told me she'd write. I've been expecting a letter." She let the sentence trail off into an unseen wasteland.

"Did you see who she left with?"

"Well, I did but I didn't." She wrinkled up her nose and turned her head sideways as she looked at me, much like a robin eyeing a suspicious worm.

I choked down my impatience. Twenty questions was getting old, but the girl was the best lead I had. "What do you mean, you did but you didn't? Surely you either saw them or you didn't."

Maria twisted her head again and rolled her eyes. If she kept up the neck twisting, either her head was going to pop off or she was going to end up screwing her neck down to her shoulders. Her hands fidgeted with a stack of credit card slips, fingers ruffling through the stack without direction or meaning.

"We… It was like this, you see. A Chinese, Japanese kind of guy picked her up. He was driving this big long stretch limo. I think it was one of those Lincoln Towncars. I mean, it was before they added to it. It was forest green with tinted windows so you couldn't see inside. But when this foreign fellow opened the door for Melissa, I could see another man's pants and shoes. I didn't think the car belonged to the little fellow; it was just too much car for such a little guy. Not that size is everything. I've known some small people who were real dynamos. Not this guy, though. You could just tell by looking at him, the way he stood, the way he carried himself that he wasn't anybody special. Just something about him. You knew right away that he was just somebody else's flunky." She shrugged her shoulders. "Simply a chauffeur." The smile on her lips was apologetic.

They had headed west she said, and she hadn't seen them since. I thanked her and left her with her pile of papers and her chipped heart. As I made my way across the lobby I wondered in which category she had pigeonholed me.

CHAPTER 8

Her long black eyelashes brushed against my cheek like an affectionate butterfly. I felt her soft, full lips against my rough, thin, chapped ones. Breath sweet as a baby's, breasts warm and inviting as they pressed against my chest, gentle hands caressing the flat ridges of stomach muscle.

She was whispering into my ear. The words were so very important, but though I strained, I couldn't quite make them out. They were just on the other side of the thin veil that separates understanding from uncertainty. It seemed as though I were trying to hear underwater, everything was distorted and rippled to me in slow motion. I raised my head to try and get closer, but she kept slipping farther and farther away. A growing sense of concern invaded my senses, and I struggled even harder to hear the faint whispers.

I could hear fear in the undecipherable words, and tears of frustration welled up in my eyes. Unseen tentacles constrained my arms. My own roar of rage rang in my ears, and my pulse pounded like a pneumatic-jackhammer at my temples.

I woke up drenched in sweat. It took me a few seconds to get my bearings. Room 14 at the Pueblo de Bandas looked old and tired in the harsh light of early morning. I disengaged myself from the tangled sheets and padded across the smooth, still cool stone floor to the narrow casement window that opened to the sounds of Carson Circle. Traffic was still light at this hour, only a dull hum on the far side of the low adobe wall that fenced in the property. Out of the right corner of my field of vision, I could see Juan raking the gravel at the back of the parking lot. I needed a shave, a cup of strong, smoking coffee and some piece of mind. Room 14 had none of those this morning. I went in search of my pants, a clean shirt, and Sergeant Nichols.

*　　*　　*

He had a head like a horse and his breath smelled like the back of a buffalo. The plastic name plate on his stainless steel desk said Nichols. The lines and crevices that traversed the leathered hide of his face spoke of more than forty years in the wind and the sand and the sun. Even his eyes were a washed out blue, as though the color had been leeched out by too many ultraviolet rays.

Nichols stared down at the slim silver pen he had wedged between the thick sausages that he passed off as fingers. He seemed a little perplexed, as though he wasn't sure why the pen was there. If the frown that rippled across his broad brow was an accurate barometer, he wasn't happy with my question.

"Yeah, sure, I remember the Gibson girl." His voice was sandpaper with a load of fine gravel sliding across it. "Blonde, purple mountain majesty eyes, and a figure just starting to ripen like grapes on the vine. Hard to forget her mother too for that matter. A real bitch. Course I couldn't really blame her. If I couldn't find my kid I'd want some help too. Course, she couldn't understand why the Santa Fe Police Department couldn't devote at least two men full-time to a search for Melissa. I tried to explain that a girl Melissa's age could do just about what she wanted as long as she stayed on the right side of the law." He smiled wanly and shrugged his massive shoulders about an inch.

"You looked for her though." I phrased it as a statement rather than a question.

"Sure we looked." He flipped me a quick glance with his washed out eyes, too quick for me to discern any hidden meaning. "You know me, Ward, I always look for the kids. Find a hell of a lot of them too," he added in a slightly defensive tone.

Find them all except your own, I thought to myself. "Call me Sanchez, Rico Sanchez. And yeah, I know you look. Maybe more than is good for you."

"More than is good for me? What the hell do you know about what's good for me, Rico Sanchez? Rico Sanchez, my ass. Loco Sanchez would be more like it. Where in God's green earth did you ever get the idea that you could go around changing your name whenever it suited you?"

He snorted in derision and flipped the pen at his desk calendar. It missed and went skittering across the floor. I turned my head and watched it slide across the linoleum and come to rest with a crash against the baseboard, but didn't make any move to go and pick it up.

"Not that it's any of your goddamn business, but I can call myself whatever the hell I want, and right now I want to call myself Sanchez." Instantly I regretted my tone. Nichols shouldn't have to suffer over my heartaches. "Sorry," I said by way of an apology. "And thanks for the referral."

He shrugged my thanks away and fidgeted with a paper clip, the long thick fingers moving with surprising quickness. Hank Nichols was not a man to cross.

23

"How many years has it been, Hank?"

"Too goddamn many," was all he said, but I knew what he meant.

Hank Nichols and I went back more than a few years. We had both been on the force in Vegas, even rode the same squad car for a time. I got sick of the glitz and the glamour and headed to Taos. Hank was more of a company man and he stayed. I lost my desire to wear the uniform, but Hank lost much more: his wife and son.

One day while he was on duty, his six-year-old son was snatched from the park where he and his mother were spending the morning. Hank went a little crazy when he heard the news. He worked virtually around the clock for three days before Linda, then his wife, called me. I drove all night to get there. I got him drunk, then sober. Together, we went all out. Two days later, we hit pay dirt. But it was too late. We found a hacked up little body and two convicted child molesters who had been paroled from California less than a month before. They never came to trial. My statement corroborated every word of Hank's story.

Hank never quit blaming Linda. He never accused her directly, but we talked about it once or twice and it was easy enough to read between the lines. She moved out less than two months later. Hank lived hard and mean for six more months then blew out of town like a Texas twister. He faxed in his resignation from Albuquerque and stopped moving in Santa Fe. I had called him a couple of times, once I tracked him down, but he wasn't talking. I hadn't set eyes on him in almost five years.

Five years can work on a man, and it sure as hell had aged Hank Nichols. The lines in his face were as deeply etched as if a leatherworker's awl had carved them out. The hair was short, gray iron filings imbedded in his scalp. Crow's feet danced around his eyes, and there was a permanent panel of pain half hidden behind his eyes.

I pushed the mists of the past aside and brought the reality of the moment into the open. "What happened, Hank? What happened to Melissa?"

He gave me a look I couldn't read and shrugged his shoulders. His cannonball of a head covered with the short gray spikes after looked like the afterbirth of a nuclear war. "Who knows? Kids today, who can figure them? They live in their own little world on their own little timetable and they answer to God knows who? I know I can't begin to get a handle on most of them, even when they are straight. Not that that happens very often."

"Was Melissa on drugs?"

"She was on something a couple of times when I saw her. Matter of fact, I should have busted her at least once, but it was only a very little grass, so I gave her the Dutch Uncle lecture and hauled her to a halfway place for teens." Hank's face dissolved into his version of a hound dog. "Turns out, maybe I should have hauled her in."

"When was she last seen?"

Hank pulled out a coffee stained manila folder. His thick fingers ruffled the pages. "It was on a Tuesday, exactly one week before her mother called."

"Who saw her?"

"Some friends, or at least acquaintances, of hers. A boy and a girl, a little older than Melissa. I think his name was Whitaker. They were living together in a studio apartment over on Woodford. They let Melissa crash on the floor a few times when she couldn't make it back to her room at the Inn of the Governors for whatever reason, must have been rather crowded."

"How was her mood that last time?"

Nichols gave me a funny look, made me feel like I was under suspicion. "You must be getting psychic or lucky in your old age, Ward. They said she was really upbeat, in a good mood. Told them she had finally found what she had been looking for her whole life. How did you know? You know something I don't?"

"Nope. Just get a feeling sometimes." I rose and headed for the door. Halfway there, I turned and gave Nicholas a casual salute. "Thanks. And by the way, the name is now Sanchez, Rico Sanchez."

I left him tolling his head sadly, a giant round cannonball of a bell. The expression on his leathery face said he was half ready to give up on me. I didn't tell him that he should have given up all the way a long time ago.

CHAPTER 9

The exposed wooden beams, darkened with age and oil, plowed furrows across the low ceiling of my modest bedroom. I lay on my back and counted eight of them. Glancing out through the narrow, almost medieval window, I could see the deep shadows of late afternoon slide smoothly across the sparse grass of what passed for a lawn and begin to seductively caress the Virginia creeper that bloomed outside my back door. A little brown bird whirled through the gathering dusk to a low limbed perch on the mesquite that grew just beyond the adobe wall that formed the rear guard of the Pueblo de Bandas. He trilled furiously for a moment extended in time, whether for his missing mate or against the coming night I couldn't decide. I picked up the black telephone receiver and dialed Gloria Gibson's number, which I had jotted down in my notebook.

She answered on the third ring, panting softly. "Hello." The way she said the word made it almost more of a question than a greeting.

"Sanchez here."

"Oh." She sounded slightly disappointed. "I thought it might be Melissa."

"Why, has she called?" Maybe this case would be over before it got started. I didn't know whether to be hacked off, or relieved.

"No, I haven't heard from her. It's just that every time the phone rings my pulse pounds a little quicker. You know, thinking that it might be her." The line hummed in a companionable sort of way as she fell silent. I waited. In another moment she spoke again. "How are you coming, Mr. Sanchez?" Her lips had trouble with my name, more likely because of psychological difficulties than physical ones.

"Making some progress. At least I've tracked down some people who know her. When you two talked, did she ever mention a guy named Mike Brown?"

The line hummed a little more while Gloria considered my question. Actually, at times, the hum was more like a whimper, as though some injured animal or maybe the wind had gotten inside the wires. "No," she said softly. "I don't believe she ever did. Why?"

26

"Just a man I ran across here in Santa Fe who she shared some conversation and a couple of drinks with."

"What sort of conversation?" Perhaps it was my imagination, but Ms. Gibson sounded just a touch apprehensive.

"Bar room talk mostly. Although he did tell me that Melissa told him that she was looking for someone, a man. Said she showed him a picture."

"What man?" she asked sharply.

"Brown didn't know him. Said he was a nice looking guy with a head full of dark hair. In the photo Melissa showed Brown, the man was wearing a light-colored suit with a striped tie. Brown said the guy looked to be in his thirties, but the picture had some age and a few smudges and creases."

"Oh no," Gloria groaned.

"What's the matter?"

"She's back on it again." Frustration and disgust gurgled in Gloria's voice.

"Back on what?" I asked, seeking enlightenment.

"That silly girl is looking for her father. I recognize the picture from your description. Let me explain. He walked out on us when Melissa was five. She's had a fixation on finding him ever since she was old enough to really realize what happened. It's been bad since she became a teenager, but it got really bad when she turned sixteen. She took all her birthday money and savings and hired a detective. There wasn't a lot of money, and it ran out after a week or so. Naturally, he never got anywhere. It was a very disappointing experience for Melissa. I thought that she had gotten over the finding Daddy syndrome, but obviously not."

"Had she been talking about him a lot lately?"

"No, dammit. She hadn't said a thing for the past several months. I never dreamed she still harbored hopes of finding the jerk." The pain and anger were still there, just below the surface, even after all the years.

"Why did he leave?"

"Why does any son of a bitch leave? I don't honestly know. We never talked about him after he left. He only called twice in all these years. Once, the first Christmas, then the night Melissa turned sixteen. He talked to her both times. Never said a word about where he was, how he was doing, or anything. After the first six months, I didn't care."

"Had you two been fighting?"

"Some, but not more than most. I stayed awake nights for months thinking about why. Never did come to any conclusion. I really don't believe there was another woman. If there was, he hid it remarkably well. He drank a little too much and bet the ponies from time to time, but those aren't reasons to leave your wife and five year old little girl." She paused,

27

then spoke words wrapped in the pent-up anger of the years. "Who knows if he even had any reasons. Most of you bastards don't."

The receiver clicked in my ear. I sat for a moment listening to the not unpleasant hum on the line, wondering where I fit in her world.

CHAPTER 10

Woodford was a pleasant middle-aged street made narrow by the cars and pickup trucks that lined both curbs. The homes were modest, mostly aluminum siding, and starting to slide from middle class authority to genteel poverty. Several needed a fresh coat of paint on the trim, and two or three needed significant repairs. The children playing on the still well-kept lawns were split almost evenly between white and Hispanic.

I finally found a parking place between a new red Toyota pickup and a big silver Lincoln Towncar that was starting to rust. I was a good two blocks beyond my destination of 517A and meandered slowly down the cracked sidewalk trying to get a feel for the neighborhood, and then, by osmosis, why Melissa had come and gone.

A boy with sleep still in his eyes and a paintbrush in his right hand answered the door after the second ring. He pushed a hank of tousled brown hair off his forehead and asked, with a touch of exasperation, if he could help me.

"Are you Ralph Whitaker?"

"Yes," he answered cautiously. Then added as an afterthought, "Who are you?"

"My name is Sanchez and I'm looking for a young girl named Melissa Gibson." I emphasized the word young, hoping to put the taste of fear in Ralph's mouth. He couldn't have been more than nineteen or twenty himself.

The hank of hair had fallen back across his forehead so that he had to look out through some of the longer strands to see me. He reminded me a bit of a young lion peering through the jungle growth. "Are you the police?"

"No, I'm private, working for Melissa's mother. However, I have just come from Sergeant Nichols' office." The boy clearly remembered the name and seemed to shrink back into the hall. I pressed my advantage. "May I come in?" I asked, putting my shoulder to the door.

He offered no resistance, stepping back instead into the narrow chamber that served as both foyer and front parlor. He held the paintbrush before him as either a sword or a talisman to ward off evil spirits like myself.

"Sergeant Nichols said you knew Melissa?"

29

The boy turned his head and cast a wistful eye about the small main room. There was nobody there to help him; only an unmade bed with twisted sheets, a thirteen inch television on a rickety stand, a pile of magazines leaned haphazardly against the wall, and a large easel. A canvas half full of yellow, orange, and red geometric designs tilted off center against the easel. I couldn't begin to tell whether it was barely half done or nearly finished. Beyond the easel was the kitchen, separated from the front room by a counter that looked as though it served as a breakfast table. Two doors were closed on either side of the hall. The one on the left was almost certainly a closet, the one on the right I figured for the bathroom. The voice of Elton John, singing a song I didn't recognize, drifted in from the kitchen and mingled with a pungent odor that I did.

"Yeah, I knew her a little bit. That's not a crime is it?" He asked his question sullenly, not really expecting an answer.

"No, Ralph, knowing her is not a crime, but withholding information about a missing girl is."

I could easily read his murky green eyes. He was asking himself whether or not he ought to tell me what he knew. I tried to help him make the right decision. "Your cooperation would be greatly appreciated, otherwise the police might become very interested in the substance you're smoking."

His eyes flashed to the ashtray sprinkled with the remains of a marijuana cigarette, then whipped back to me. Even before he spoke I could tell that I had said the wrong thing, a trait which I'd acquired early in life.

"Get out, you fucking narc." The muscle in his jaw worked in anger. He flipped the hair back out of his eyes and waved the brush about furiously in the air.

I leaned back out of the arc of the brush. "I'm not a narc."

"Get out. Get the hell out of my place."

"Listen, Ralph, I'm sorry for what I said. I was out of line, but Melissa's mother is very concerned. She hasn't heard from her in nearly two weeks, and Melissa has always been very conscientious about calling. You're the best lead I have. Won't you help? Melissa may be in big trouble."

"Too damn bad. You're trespassing. Now get out before I have to throw you out." He flexed a rather flabby bicep at me.

I wasn't worried in the least about Ralph's right, or his left for that matter, but I wasn't going to get anywhere with him in such a state. I gave Ralph a dirty look that I probably should have reserved for myself and retreated slowly to the sidewalk, where I spent an unproductive five minutes looking at the front of 517A and reevaluating the situation.

Seeing no point in making a further spectacle of myself, I trekked back to my car, castigating myself with every step for my inept handling of the situation. The morning sun streaming through the windshield only served to make me hotter as I slid behind the wheel.

I was so busy giving myself mental hell that I nearly didn't see her. She was a skinny dishwater blonde going brown at the roots. She stepped from her post at the end of a long line of gray metal trash cans and flagged me down. I had to slam on the brakes to keep from running over her.

Her small breasts pressed against the thin Lakers T-shirt that hung down well below her waist. Her jeans were full of holes and she was barefoot, but concern lit up her mud brown eyes. "Are you the detective?"

"Yes. Who are you?"

"I'm Angela, Ralph's girl," she explained. "You're the one that is trying to find Melissa?" Her eyes roved anxiously toward the curtained windows of 517A. "I was in the bathroom and heard you talking to Ralph. He's a good guy, but you scared him when you started talking about the police. He's had a couple of run-ins with them already and he is really sensitive about the subject."

"Yeah, I noticed. I've got a big mouth and sometimes I stick my foot in it." I followed her glance back again to the room. "Are you okay?"

She moved her head in quick, nervous little nods. "Yeah. It's just that Ralph would kill me if he caught me talking to you right now."

I motioned at the passenger door. "Get in. I'll drive around the block a couple of times, give you a chance to talk."

"I can't, I've got to get back in before Ralph gets out of the shower. He's probably about through by now. It took you forever to get back," she said accusingly. "I was ready to go back in when I saw you coming."

"Sorry, I'm slowing down in my old age. Did you want to talk to me about Melissa?"

"It wasn't much." Her voice trailed off into a thicket of uncertainties.

"Go on, talk. You must have thought that it was important or you wouldn't have come down."

I watched the big lump in her throat go down and back up. She gave me a wan smile. "You're right. I wanted to tell you that I saw Melissa about three days ago."

"Where?" I deliberately tried to keep the excitement down in my voice. The girl was as nervous as a young doe. I didn't need to frighten her off like I had Ralph.

"She was in a big limo outside the A&P on Sacramento. I couldn't see anybody else in the back, but there was this little Chinese or Japanese guy with a chauffeur's hat up front. I wanted to go over and say hello, but I felt real funny about going up to her when she was in that big limo. I figured maybe Melissa wouldn't want me to bother her. I always knew when she spent the night with us that she didn't belong here." Her glance took in

Woodford Street and the lower middle class world she represented. "Anyway, it was real early in the morning and the windows were tinted, so I couldn't be absolutely positive it was her." Her eyes belied her words. She was very sure.

Suddenly Ralph's voice cut through the quiet. "Angela."

Her hand was suddenly soft on my arm. "I've got to go. Please find Melissa. She has everything going for her—looks, talent, money. I know I'll never amount to much, but Melissa can. I want her to have a chance."

Angela's slender fingers tightened for a instant on my arm, and then she was gone, her bare feet flying across the pavement, rear end as skinny and firm as a teenage boy's. With a degree of fondness, I watched her bound up the steps to 517A two at a time. I wasn't at all sure she was correct in her self-assessment. Ralph's tousled head, still damp from the shower, protruded from his fortress. I slid down below the window level. I didn't want to spoil Angela's dreams of happiness, even if they were centered on a character like Ralph. After all, maybe he wasn't so terrible. Only terribly young.

CHAPTER 11

I found the A&P just after noon. No place else to go, nothing else to do, so I maneuvered my vehicle into a semi-shady parking space, rolled down my window, and prepared to wait. The rear end of my Jeep almost nudged the white painted concrete block that served as the extension and I was only four spaces from the entrance, half-covered by the shade created by the building itself. It was an ideal spot, and I settled myself down for a long wait. He might come later this afternoon, tomorrow, or not at all. However, unless I got an unexpected flash of brilliance, I had to wait. This was my only lead.

The afternoon began with a promise that faded as the minutes slowly melted into hours. As the lengthening shadows of the afternoon submerged my vehicle, I watched the shoppers come and go. Nobody was particularly ugly or beautiful, nor did they buy a lot. A couple of young mothers had nearly full carts, but most of the customers were older with limited appetites, or budgets; one- or two-baggers.

Even with the ever-growing shadows and the windows all rolled down, it was quite warm in my vehicle. About four-thirty the feeble breeze that had puffed periodically across the parking lot petered out completely. In five minutes I could feel the sweat forming a swimming pool in the small of my back. Five minutes later I was mopping at the beads trickling down my forehead from the hairline. After three hundred more seconds I got out of the car and went to get a Coke out of the phalanx of brightly colored machines that guarded the front of the store. The asphalt parking lot was mushy beneath my hiking boots.

In my youth, I would have purchased a Diet-Rite; they used to burn most pleasantly all the way from your throat to your stomach. However, today's version tasted to me like mildly flavored colored water. Diet Cokes don't really turn my crank either, but I dropped in two quarters anyway.

I took the chilled aluminum can and went and sat on a wooden bench located just to the left of the automatic doors. Companies had paid to have their advertisements painted on the slats. There were advertisements for a pizza place, a bakery, a bookstore, two insurance agencies, and a funeral parlor. After ten minutes I felt like I was waiting for Godot, or the last bus to Bakersfield.

As far back as I can remember, I have never particularly liked living with or being close to any one person. People when viewed from a distance, or at least with a great deal of detachment, aren't nearly as bad. I sipped aluminum flavored soda on a wooden bench in the hot New Mexico sun and watched the world go by. Nobody spoke to me except for a old Mexican man who asked if I had the time and a dirty faced little girl of about six who was dressed in a dusty white dress and wanted to know if I had seen her mommy.

I told the old man it was five fifteen; I didn't have to answer the little girl because she suddenly spied her mommy coming out the door with an aggrieved expression. The little girl scampered across the pavement. Mom greeted the child with a sharp smack on each bare leg, then picked her up and carried her back into the store, casting a hateful look over her shoulder in my general direction.

The afternoon was getting a bit frazzled around the edges, and I didn't want any trouble with a scared mother already mad at herself for losing track of her child, so I escorted myself to the far side of the black softening asphalt and sat down in the shade of a pinion tree. The day died slowly in a golden glory in the western sky, but I never saw a Lincoln of any color. When the sky was as black as the asphalt, I got back in my car and headed for a McLean Deluxe and the Pueblo de Bandas. Another day in Paradise. Another day survived.

*   *   *

Deep in the bowels of the night, I awoke to the sounds of something scurrying, either across the floor or across the floor of my mind. I sat upright in the soft mushiness of the worn mattress, heart racing, anger surging. Mad at myself for being so frightened by a field mouse or a dream. I banged my head back against the unadorned adobe wall that rose behind my bed and tried to remember the last time I had been frightened.

I really didn't have to try very hard, and I knew that. I knew the time, the place, the exact moment when it happened. I had revisited the event a hundred times waking and dreaming. I could tell anyone who cared to listen every vivid, horrible detail. To tell the truth, I came back not so much to revisit as to mourn. It was as though I returned to an old shrine, or to pick at an old scab.

I hadn't been afraid since that September moment when I peered over the edge of the narrow sandstone ledge and saw the brilliant red and gold dress sprawled on the rocky creek bank below. I knew the minute I saw.

34

Knew that she was dead. It wasn't a question of if; there wasn't a doubt in my mind. Maybe it was the way her neck was twisted, or the coppery pool that formed beneath her mass of soft brown hair. I don't think there was any scientific or even logical reason. I just was certain, deep in my heart or soul or gut, where no one is ever wrong, that Sharon was dead.

I was also just as certain that, in some way, I was to blame. I didn't push her, at least not physically, but I wasn't there when she really needed me.

The sheriff looked long and hard, I'll give him that, and I looked longer and harder, but neither of us was ever able to conclusively prove whether she slipped or jumped, or was pushed. The blowing sands, the remoteness of the area, and my own selfishness combined to render us helpless at every turn. The final legal verdict was an accident; I sentenced myself to an eternity of shame.

The smooth adobe walls were cool to the touch, but my body felt like it was being consumed by an internal flame. Traffic was light on Carson Circle; a police car went by about two-thirty headed south, followed ten minutes later by a taxi going the same way. It gleamed yellow in the pool of light that fell from the street lamp and I half wished I was in the back seat. A little after three, a rattletrap of a faded green pickup sputtered by, headed north. About four o'clock, the adobe closed in too tightly on me and I went and put on my running shorts and an old pair of Asics.

Nobody tried to stop me as I slipped over the top of the wall at the back of the compound and slid down the short bank of loose sandy dirt that separated Pueblo de Bandas from Carson Circle. I hadn't run in almost two weeks and I hadn't run on pavement in almost two years. The asphalt jarred my joints and my shoes sounded like a herd of buffalo in the quiet pre-dawn. I ran south toward Mexico.

In less than five minutes, the neighborhood began to change. Houses were no longer well kept and what weeds could grow in the semi-arid climate had fought their way through the crust of the soil and held forth in the yards and entwined themselves on fading wrought iron fences and rusting heaps of metal that used to be automobiles. Houses gave way to second hand clothing stores, corner groceries, darkened store fronts, and bars where the cleaning crew swabbed at filthy linoleum with ragged mops and dirty water. A dog rushed against the fence as I crossed Chastain, barking and growling and making the chainlink rattle like mad. I paid him no more mind than I did the carbon monoxide spewing city bus that passed by rolling north toward the center of town. I heard only the wind inside my own head whirling all the insanities of the moment together in a cyclone of craziness that drove me on. I ran on. I ran south toward Mexico. I ran to escape the moment and mankind, but most of all, myself.

*   *   *

There is a peace which comes for a brief moment after a mad rush when a man's defenses are down and his tenses are suspended. It was this state that very nearly caused me to miss the Lincoln. I had lingered too long with Juan over a second cup of nasty black coffee in the courtyard of the Pueblo de Bandas and as a consequence had had to make like a madman to make it to the A&P when they opened at seven. Angela had made her sighting very early in the morning. Maybe that was a pattern.

In the moment of suspended sensory alertness, I had closed my eyes and the waves of blackness rushed in behind them and lapped at the ends of my jagged nerves. It had been a long night and a short one.

When I opened them the limo was already there, more black than green in the shadowy blush of first daylight. It was pulled up parallel to the door and a girl in a soft green dress was already halfway through the automatic door.

Seconds moved like minutes, slow molasses minutes in the moribund timepiece of my mind. At three minutes I was antsy. At four, I was drumming my fingers on the dashboard. At five, my hand was on the door handle. I told myself to count to ten—no point in upsetting the equilibrium unnecessarily.

I had reached six when she came out the door, a plastic sack in each hand.

She wasn't Melissa; at least not the Melissa whose photograph I had seen. She was dark in a Hispanic way and shorter than the description her mother had given me. Her breasts were full and her round little tummy pressed against the fabric of her dress. Her legs were good and her lips were beautifully formed. Her lip gloss was the color of Indian Paintbrush. No, she wasn't Melissa, but she was worth a second look. More to the point, she got in the front seat of the limo.

I counted to fourteen and followed the Lincoln out of the parking lot. Santa Fe isn't New York or Los Angeles, but morning rush hour was still heavy. The long green Lincoln stood out though like a pine tree on the Sahara. I let the limo get a couple of blocks ahead and then gradually closed the gap until there was only a blue Corvette and a motorcycle between me and the Lincoln. I had a bad moment when I caught the light at Sedona, but I gunned the motor and caught them again at Preston. We lost the motorcycle at the new Wal-Mart and the Vette at a Hardee's. When the Lincoln turned left onto Colorado Canyon Road, I let it go and went up two blocks before I turned left on Bridger. Then I raced up two more blocks, took a left on Greenleaf, and two blocks later slid back in behind the Lincoln.

We rolled along at forty-five for about two miles and then he turned down a private lane. I went up another half mile and made a U-turn, my tires spinning in the soft sand spread along the edge of the road. As I watched the dust settle courtesy of my rearview mirror, I debated with myself on the merits of following now or coming back after dark. Then I was back at the private road and had to make one of those split-second decisions that often lead you far from the path of righteousness. I spun the wheel and turned right.

I had been on several of these private lanes that spread out from Santa Fe like the spokes of an old, abandoned wagon wheel, beginning together at the hub but bound at the outer rim only by the desert. They usually went for only a half or three quarters of a mile. It wasn't that the paving was so difficult, it was just too damn expensive to run the water lines any further out. This one wound slowly up a steep grade with great wide sweeping turns like the path of a drunken snake. After about a quarter mile, there was a sudden outcropping of reddish rock. I made another U-turn and backed carefully off the road until my bumper almost caressed the stones. The nose of my vehicle was pointed back toward Colorado Canyon Road.

Without the breeze stirred up by the moving car, it was already a warm New Mexico morning. I sat for a few minutes, arranging my thoughts in some semblance of order and developing a scheme of attack. Before I worked out all the variables, the inside of the car became an oven. I put my keys in my pocket and stepped outside.

There were no clouds that morning, no trees or bushes grew on the rocky outcropping, nothing between me and the brilliant sun. It beamed down upon me without mercy, which in truth I probably did not deserve. I longed for some water, but was grateful for my Yankees baseball cap. I picked my way carefully through the rapidly warming stones. For some stupid reason, I had worn an old pair of running shoes and already, through their thin soles, I could feel the warmth of the sand that lay like a meager blanket across the top of most of the rocky ledge.

It took me ten minutes to carefully pick my way up and down the ledge. On the far side I could see a great stone fence, and beyond that, a long, low-slung ranch house of pale red brick topped by a flat slate roof of a deeper red. There were two hundred yards of open ground between the end of my rocks and the wall. The only cover was a small copse of cottonwoods and mesquite that lay to my left and straggled along for better than a hundred yards. However, the trees gave out fifty yards from the fence, and worse, there were thirty yards of naked ground broken only by a pair of cactus and one stray boulder between me and the beginning of the cover.

I lingered in the shade cast by the last of the big boulders and thought about my options. Several minutes later I decided that the cover was worth the risk; anyway, anything beat being sun dried on a rock pile. I crossed my fingers and started running.

I made the trees in a series of short sprints, going straight when there was cover close ahead, zigzagging with the grain of the sand drifts when there was not, but staying low to the scorching earth at all times.

No one shouted, no rifle shots split the air; all I could hear was my own rapid, shallow breathing and the scurrying sounds of some small unseen creature as it sought the shelter of its own burrow. I moved carefully but steadily among the trees, pausing every few feet to hear if my approach had been discovered. All was quiet on the western front.

At the edge of the grove I paused for several minutes to reconnoiter. If I listened carefully, I could catch unintelligible snatches of conversation and foreshortened peals of laughter. My watch said ten-thirty when I made my last mad dash to the wall. I sat with my back against the heated stones for several minutes, catching my breath and wondering what in the hell I was going to do next.

What I did was sit and think for twenty minutes. I was trying to come up with a foolproof plan to get over the wall and down the other side without being seen. The wall itself wasn't going to be too tough. It was four, maybe five feet high and appeared to be about as thick as the waist of an average man. No, getting over the wall wasn't the problem; getting over the wall without getting caught, now that was the problem. There was too much open ground, little if any cover, and not much chance for a diversion. The worst of it was I didn't know what was going to be there to greet me on the other side of the stones. My imagination produced scenes of Dobermans and machine pistols. I began to wonder if I shouldn't be thinking up a good story for whomever owned the place.

My thinking didn't produce any great ideas or even an interesting storyline. It also didn't get me any closer to getting over the wall. I was getting more hot and thirsty by the minute. I didn't want to wait until dark, and I'd come too far to turn back, so I gathered my fading, foolhardy resolve and carefully slid one hand up the side of the rough stones and began to stand up. I was going to feel extremely stupid if Melissa wasn't even here. After all, I was hanging way out in space tethered only to a very thin thread.

Eyeball high to the top of the wall I paused and peered over the side. I was lucky, very lucky. By pure chance I had picked a spot that backed up to what appeared to be the garage of the house. It was solid brick and windowless on my side. I could see part of the driveway curving away and what looked like a blue Ford Expedition. No sign of the green Lincoln, but then I could see only a small percentage of the driveway and none of the inside of the garage. I took a deep breath and dragged myself up and over the wall. The jagged edges of the rocks scraped at the skin of my palms and the landing jarred me to my hips, but there were no shrill alarms, no barking dogs, no small arms fire. I duck-walked across the twenty feet to the back of the garage.

I put my back up against the bricks and listened to my own rapid breathing. Soon I began to hear other noises. I could hear playful shouting and feminine peals of laughter. There was music, and occasionally the splash of water. The sounds were coming from beyond the far end of the long house. I began to work my way toward those sounds.

Low and slow was the way to go, and except for a bad moment when I spooked a small lizard and another when I had to cross in front of a large glass patio door, I didn't have any trouble. In less than five minutes I had reached the end of the house. The laughter and splashing were louder now. Like a suspicious old turtle, I cautiously stuck my head around the corner of the building.

Pool party time in Santa Fe. My first brief glance had revealed a half dozen or so young girls clad only in bikinis, and at least three men dressed in sport shirts and slacks. Two of them were holding guns. I held my cheek tight against the rough bricks and shivered in the sweltering heat.

CHAPTER 12

Dead or alive, Elvis still sounded good, especially after listening to Michael Jackson for the past twenty minutes. I had been glad when somebody had switched the CDs. From the snatches of conversation I could pick up it sounded like the guards had insisted that the change be made. The girl, I thought I heard them call her Jill, fussed a little but not much. Unhappy, heavily armed men with surly dispositions were not to be trifled with, even if you had a pair of overripe cantaloupes masquerading as your breasts.

It had taken me virtually an entire CD to work my way to my current vantage point. I was on the far side of the pool from where I had first entered the compound. My back was against the wall of a low slung cabana on the west side of the pool. From here I was only thirty feet from the water and I had a good view of all but the far south end of the pool. By sticking my neck out just a little I could see both of the armed men and four, sometimes five, of the girls.

One of the girls, seated in a deck chair with her back to me, had long blonde hair roughly the shade Melissa wore in the photograph I carried in my billfold. She was chatting with a short plump redhead and they were both smoking off the same off-color cigarette. Neither one had turned around my way since I had covered the final ten yards of open ground. I had mixed feelings about this lack of attention.

Right now, I wasn't looking at either the women or the two men. I was looking at my feet. I was looking at them because they were still half out in the sun. The rest of me was in fairly deep shade offered by the cabana, a half dozen scraggly mesquite trees and a trio of thick hedges trimmed to look like overgrown mushrooms. I would have hated to pay for their watering.

I also had no desire to be discovered at this point. I truly had no real business being here. I hadn't been invited, didn't know a soul, and couldn't even swear that any laws had been broken at the ranch. I had half a lead and half a hunch and was trying to add them together and make them equal five. I was way out in left field, and to tell the truth, I wasn't even sure what inning it was.

The redhead was talking now, and I could hear a hint of excitement in her voice. She wasn't talking loud enough for me to make out many of the words, although I caught something about "a bar at Reno" and "dancing at Diversions". Melissa, if it was Melissa, wasn't saying much in turn. I carefully scooted another foot closer to the pool so I could get a better look.

I was more exposed than ever. At least six inches of my lower legs and my shoes were in full sunlight, but I had a much better angle. I could now see all but the last ten feet or so of the far right end of the pool. The third gunman was gone, or at least he was no longer where he had been. I could see a half-opened sliding glass door at the edge of the patio. The interior of the house was too dark to see much, a foot and a half of Kentucky blue carpet just inside the door was highlighted by the late afternoon sun. Something brassy gleamed at the far left edge of the carpet that I could see from my angle of vision. One small sandal sat forlornly on the edge of the patio.

The music switched again, this time to a more bouncy, almost Latin rhythm. The infectious rhythm propelled the redhead from her chair. Stubby brown cigarette hanging from her lips, she began swaying to the beat. Her lime green bikini didn't cover much of the ample flesh that her bones carried. Short, not much over five feet, she was built like a much bigger girl. Her soft white breasts overflowed her top and spilled down the sides like mounds of whipping cream. She obviously hadn't spent much time outdoors in the Southwestern sun. Just as obviously, she had spent a good deal of time on some dance floor. Her movements were sensuous and surprisingly graceful, her arms elegant, her legs well-made and muscular. Even though she was packing ten extra pounds around her middle, she was still delivering a truckload of uninhibited sexual intensity.

Her dancing caught the attention of the two guards. I could see them both clearly now as they wandered a few steps closer toward her side of the pool. Unfortunately, that was my side as well. There were two of them; a tall slender reed of a man in a pale blue sports shirt, off-white slacks, and a long barreled shotgun with a polished walnut stock that gleamed in the late afternoon sun, and a short dark man with a bushy black mustache, a nasty expression on a face full of acne craters, and enough grease on his slick-backed hair to raise an environmentalist's blood pressure at least twenty points. The nasty black machine pistol dangling from his left hand glistened just like his greasy hair. I scrunched a little closer to the rough bricks of the cabana. Their rough particles were needles in my back.

"Do it, Lisa!" shouted short and dark. He had a Mexican accent with a faint, peculiar lisp.

The redhead turned her head and gave him a look of disgust over the top of her pert nose. For no particular reason I noted a band of freckles that marched up one side of that little nose and down the other. Those innocent brown spots didn't seem to be in harmony with the mounds of jiggling flesh and the lethal weapons. There was no aura of innocence about this fortress in the desert; it was a place that meant business. I was getting strong undercurrents that it was not legitimate commerce.

"Come on, babe, give me a thrill." He moved his bowlegs another step closer to the enticing flesh.

"Shut up, Luis." Lisa's voice was little girl, long spoiled. The blonde on the other lounge chair turned to look at Luis. If it wasn't Melissa, I wasn't in a hot dangerous place. The reed leaned against a metal ladder that descended into the pool on his end and dug a pack of Marlboros out of his shirt pocket with his left hand. The right hand caressed the twin barrels of his shotgun. He stuck a cigarette in his mouth and lit it with a ninety-nine cent Bic lighter. His eyes never left the redhead and his right hand never left the shotgun.

"Don't tell me what to do, you cunt." Luis' lisp was incongruous with his snarl. "I don't take no orders from no fuckin' cunt." He raised a hand as though he would slap her from twenty feet. The machine pistol it held scared the hell out of me.

"Luis, you don't want any part of me. Mr. Miller will take you, you dumb Mexican son of a bitch." She had stopped her dancing and stood half bent at the waist, pounds of creamy flesh tumbling out in the direction of Luis. The cigarette lay forgotten on the damp concrete. Melissa was propped up on one elbow, a bemused smile on her face. Wraparound sunglasses hid her purple eyes, but I was certain I had found her.

Luis took two quick steps toward Lisa, and she beat a hasty retreat, breasts bouncing like twin basketballs out of control. "Shut the fuck up," he growled, "or I'll teach you a lesson you won't soon forget. As for Miller," he spat in the general direction of the pool, "I'll—"

"You'll what, Luis?" a silky smooth male voice interrupted.

Luis stopped in mid-sentence and mid-stride. He turned sharply toward the voice. "Nothing, Mr. Miller. I was just, well, you know." Luis' head hung down like an egg-sucking dog. The machine pistol dangled loosely from his fingers. I shot a quick glance at the thin man. He might have been standing a little more erect but otherwise appeared unmoved. Smoke from his Marlboro curled around his narrow face. I looked back toward the house; that was where the voice was.

The voice was attached to the tall man who stepped out the patio door and walked directly toward my side of the pool. His hair was a silver mane that framed his deeply tanned face and curled profusely on the back of his neck. He wore Oakley sunglasses, gray dress slacks, and a white Izod sports shirt. A gold chain as thick as my thumb hung across his upper chest, a gold

Rolex gripped his left wrist, and his pinkie ring looked to be a large ruby. His tasseled loafers were as black and shiny as jet. He walked with purpose and pride, as if he owned the place. I figured he probably did.

The swimming pool crowd watched him closely, so I did too. The closer he got to my side of the pool the more his age showed. I had put him in his early forties when he first came out the door, however, now I could see that I was off a dozen years, or more. His deep tan, slim body and carefully styled hair were his smoke and mirrors. He was mid-fifties, maybe pushing sixty with the style that maturity sometimes brings, or that enough money can provide. Another man, taller, thinner, and a touch less well-dressed, followed about five paces behind like a scavenger fish following a great white shark. He had a sleepy expression on his face that was belied by his x-ray eyes. They were gunmetal gray and cold as arctic ice. I had seen his kind before in Vegas, Reno, and L.A., he was trouble, waiting patiently for the right moment.

Miller paused alongside Luis and murmured something too low for me to hear. Luis heard him out, then turned on his heel and walked around the pool and into the house without uttering a sound. Miller gave the hangers-on at the pool a long slow once-over and they all suddenly found something very interesting to do. Mr. Big, satisfied with the state of affairs, resumed his walk around the waters. He causally strolled up to the redhead and put his arm around her as if he owned her. I took my eyes off him long enough to glance at Melissa. She was gazing up at the couple with a rapt expression. I didn't even know her and I was disappointed. Trouble had stopped about ten feet away. He slowly scanned the pool area, then the surrounding countryside. His eyes were alert and quick, dancing here, darting there. I had a feeling in my gut that a jack rabbit couldn't move out on the desert without him seeing it.

Miller posed for a camera that wasn't there, one arm around the chunky redhead, his hand rubbing gently against the side of one of her barely covered breasts. She let one small hand wander through the silver undergrowth of hair on his chest. The other one drifted south in the general vicinity of his buttocks. Something about him triggered a blurry image in my memory banks. I wanted him to take off his sunglasses so I could see his eyes. I had seen him somewhere before, either in person, on TV or in a magazine. Somewhere, I just couldn't place it.

Melissa purred syllables I couldn't hear well enough to decode. Miller disentangled himself from the redhead, leaned over at the waist, and kissed Melissa's upturned face flush on the lips. "How's my baby today?" he asked.

"Doing good," she said in a low, surprisingly throaty voice. "How about you?"

"All right, except for having to deal with some of the hired help. That Luis, if his brains were dynamite, he couldn't blow his nose." The *menage a trois* thought that was worth a laugh. Trouble never cracked a smile. He looked cool even in the heat, as if he had a core of ice at the center of his body. Perhaps it was taking the place of his heart.

Lisa couldn't stand to be the odd girl out. She squeezed into the frame, tight against Miller, breasts flattened against his back, long red hair falling down across his shoulders like copper rivulets. Her fine, even white teeth nibbled on the tanned hide at the apex of his neck and shoulder. Her hands busied themselves with his chest hair and shirt buttons.

"Wanta play?" she lisped. She nibbled harder on his neck to show how ready she was. Her hands slowly slid south.

Miller rolled his eyes at Melissa as if to say, "Look what I have to endure," but his back curved to meet the softness of her breasts. Melissa gave him a bright smile that didn't make it beyond her lips. Trouble looked as if he had seen it all before. I figured he had. Miller leaned down and gave Melissa another kiss, this one on the cheek, and patted her bare arm. She and I could see the bulge at the front of his pants. She whispered "Bye" so faintly that I might have imagined it.

Miller strolled back to the house with the redhead giving him a moving massage. Trouble gave Melissa a glassy-eyed stare that wiped the smile off her lips, then turned and followed the boss. I pulled my knees up against my chest and willed myself to be a shadow on the cabana wall.

CHAPTER 13

The sun was low in the dying sky, a blood red ball poised on the horizon. Shadows mixed with twilight in pools of blue so dark they were virtually black. A bird flew low and hard above the pool and fluttered into a Paloverde tree. Its image, marginally dark in the faded sky, was that of a dove. I wondered if it was symbolic.

The air was noticeably cooler than even an hour earlier. The pool party had been breaking up since five o'clock. People drifted off singly or in pairs. I couldn't be positive in the dense afterglow that defined the desert twilight, but I thought that only three remained in the pool area. Melissa still lay in her chair. She had been there all afternoon except once to go and get a beer and once to take what I figured was a potty break. A slim brunette, with a flat chest and show girl legs, had passed out at about four from a steady diet of Tequila Slammers. Her companion, a dark-haired girl of Asian ancestry, had tried lethargically to rouse her, then given up and gone in.

At the far end of the pool a red glow from a cigarette marked the location of the last guard. He had come on at five. Younger than the others, he had been restless at first, pacing up and down the length of the pool like a caged coyote, but he'd settled down with the coming darkness on a low stone bench that afforded him a panoramic view of the pool, the patio, and my side of the cabana. I thanked that Great Spirit for the gathering darkness and aimed for a catatonic state.

It was my time to leave; that quiet lull between the dying of the day and the arousal of the night. If I were quiet and lucky, I could be over the wall and loping across the desert in ten minutes. Even if they heard me they couldn't see me until they hit the switch for the six floodlights I had noticed earlier in the day. I figured I could still make the wall, and once over, I planned to be one tough hombre to hit. They didn't have near enough power on those poles to light up the desert, and away from the wall there was a fair amount of rocks, brush, cactus and Mexican jumping bean shrub to provide cover.

However, I couldn't leave. Not just yet; not with Melissa only twenty feet away. I had hoped to find out where she was with my crazy journey; to actually get to talk to with her was a bonus, for which I was prepared to take some big chances. All I needed was the guard to go take a leak or full darkness to fall across the pool. It had been a long wait on a hot afternoon, but I am an experienced waiter, and my ultimate destination figured to make this place seem like Antarctica. I had heard for years that only the good die young, and I was already on the backside of thirty.

*   *   *

Night fell in a rush like the final curtain after the last act of MacBeth. A hint of breeze delivered a soft promise of a kiss on my cheek. Residual heat from the day radiated from the stucco that pressed against my back like a faithful old friend. I now knew the wall intimately. The wall and all the grass and shrubs within a ten foot semi-circle.

My eyes had grown accustomed to the deepening twilight and the transition to night was no challenge. It wasn't totally dark even on the wrong side of the cabana. Light from one of the trio of towers that was positioned on the other side of my cabana spilled over onto the lawn just five feet from me. Underwater lights set at regular intervals, about every four feet, gave an eerie glow to the rectangular cement pool, a lone yellow bug light burned on the patio outside the big, sliding glass door.

The party was still going on, but it had moved to the front of the house. Leftover lights and used music drifted jointly through an open window a few feet to the right of the half open sliding glass door. A bathroom must have been located on the pool side of the house; every few minutes I could hear a urinal flush as someone relieved themselves. About twenty minutes or so after the curtain of darkness had fallen, the red glow of the cigarette at the far end of the pool moved closer to the house. Another five minutes and I could see half the guard's body as he moved to his right and into the yellow arc of the bug light. He was facing the house.

I wriggled my toes and fingers to get the blood flowing then slowly worked my way up to a standing position. I was careful to stay within the deep shadows thrown by the cabana. It was difficult to leave the perceived security afforded by the stucco wall rising against my back, but success tonight would only come to the bold. With great reluctance, I made the first cautious step toward the pool.

Three more steps and I was there, poolside, ringside, where the action and Melissa were. I kept one eye on the guard and one on the dim path in front of me. The last thing I needed was to trip over a beer bottle. The guard, engrossed in the activities in the house, never moved. The brunette twitched her long, slim legs and raised her head about six inches off the concrete, but she was too far under to do more. I paused until she dropped her head, then maneuvered around a discarded beach towel and a plastic bottle of

Coppertone. Acting like I owned the place, I slid casually and quietly into a lounge chair beside Melissa. If she noticed my arrival she didn't let it show. She was either stoned or deep in thought. There was a half full can of beer beside my chair. I picked up the can and let the half warm beer slide down my throat. I was very thirsty.

"Nice night, isn't it?"

I watched her golden hair swirl as she turned her head in the dark. She gave me a long stare but no answer. It was too dark to read her face.

I tried again. "How come you aren't inside with the rest?"

"Who sent you?" There was a certain harshness to her youthful voice.

"Someone we both know."

"Why don't you go bug them."

"You seem more interesting."

Her palomino head inclined toward me. "How would you know? I've never seen you in my life." She propped herself up on one elbow. Long distance light from the bug bulb revealed the purple eyes. "Who are you anyway?"

"The name's Sanchez."

"You don't look Hispanic."

"I'm not. What's your name?"

"Why do you want to know?"

"I'm curious."

Another long stare. I thought she wasn't going to answer, but suddenly she sighed, "Amber."

I bent forward at the waist and inched my head a little closer to her face. Her fair skin appeared sallow in the yellow light. "Funny," I whispered, "you look more like a Melissa to me."

Fear danced in her purple eyes and crawled across her cheeks. "Who are you, goddammit?"

"Your mother is very worried, Melissa."

In a heartbeat her left hand was on my arm, fingers tightening on my bicep like a python. "What do you know about my mother, you son of a bitch? What do you think you're doing coming out of the dark like some demon, trying to scare the hell out of me? If you don't have a very good explanation right now, I'm going to scream and they're going to be on you so fast you'll never know what hit you."

I wondered who they were. I shot a quick glance at the guard. He was still staring toward the interior of the house. Nonetheless, the sweat trickled from my armpit and I wished for my gun. It wasn't the first time I had that wish this day. I sighed slowly and with deep resignation to let her know I wasn't worried, and was slightly disappointed with her attitude.

47

"Melissa, your mother hasn't heard from you in quite a while. It's only natural that she be worried."

"My mother never worried about me a day in her life," she snarled. "The only things she cares about are her money and her power, so I guess she's missing her little meal ticket."

"You make money for your mother?"

"I have done lots of things for my mother, none of which are your fuckin' business." She paused and looked at me out of the sides of her eyes, like a bird looking at a half-dead worm, trying to decide it was still edible. "What is she paying you anyway? Thirty shekels of silver?"

"Nothing so biblical. The amount is not that important. What is important is that she cares enough about you to send someone to look for you. She went to a good deal of trouble to track me down. She must think you're a pretty valuable child."

"A valuable commodity is more like it."

"Aren't you a little harsh on your mother?" I was getting a bit tired of the girl's poor little picked on me attitude.

She gave me a withering look. Maybe it was the bug light, or maybe there was venom in her deep purple eyes. "You don't know anything about my mother or me. Why don't you go crawl back under whatever godforsaken rock you crawled out from under."

The guard was getting bored with being on the outside looking in. He shifted his weight from one foot to the other then drug a pack of cigarettes out of his shirt pocket and tapped out a cancer stick. I waited until the second puff of smoke coiled up around his eyes before I spoke. It was getting late for me. I didn't want to stay too long at the ball so I was direct and to the point. I wasn't wearing glass slippers. "Why don't you come with me?"

"Why would I want to?" Disgust dripped from her voice like water from an icicle in a heatwave.

"What's here for you? Your mom is at your house waiting for you to come home. You could either come with me tonight or meet me in Santa Fe tomorrow or the next day. I'll be at the Pueblo de Bandas."

"Listen, Sanchez, or whatever the hell your name is, what is here is what I've been looking for almost my whole life. Believe it or else, my mother isn't worried about me, she just misses what I can do for her. I'm doing fine, absolutely fine. For the first time in my life I'm happy. People appreciate me for who I am, not what I can do for them. You can tell my mother not to worry; her little girl found what she was looking for. No, better yet, tell her to go straight to hell, do not pass go, do not collect two hundred dollars."

I put one hand on her soft shoulder as I left, just to let her know I was there. Her skin felt hot to the touch. I leaned down and whispered the name of my hotel in her ear. Vision in the desert is an uncertain sense; lighting is often broken in the clear atmosphere as though distorted by the purity. It is difficult to see clearly and exactly during the day, nearly impossible at night. Things are often not what they seem, whether this is because the mind is controlling the eye, making it see what the brain wants to see, or whether the eye, unaccustomed to the clarity and purity of the air, overcompensates for the distortion that is the norm.

As I finished my conspiratorial whisper, I thought I saw a single silver tear slide down Melissa's left cheek. Then again, maybe it was only desert distortion syndrome.

CHAPTER 14

My body felt like a war zone the next morning. I lay in bed for a time after I awoke, letting the sunlight filter through the partings of the curtains and reviewing my varied assortment of scrapes and bruises. Romance in the purest form is a full moon over a long, low swell of desert sand. Romance and reality are almost certain to be two different distortions of the same phenomenon. Romance is how we wish it was; reality is how we make life. Neither is correct. Neither is incorrect. Like two different mirrors at the funhouse, one shows you hollow and thinner than you are, the other short and fatter. The rock and brittlebush had been there. I didn't have to run into them and fall over them, but I had.

One long scrape on my left arm and a deep purplish bruise the size of a grapefruit on my right leg looked the worst. My left knee hurt when I bent it and I had to pull at two leftover cactus spikes from my fleshy left hindquarter. No forgiveness for error from the desert at night. I stayed in bed for a good hour after waking up that morning; just taking stock of my body, then trying to make some sense out of my strange, wonderful case.

I had a little lost girl found, who wanted to stay lost. I had to admit that Gloria Gibson seemed a little hard around the edges, but Melissa had been adamant about not wanting to go home to her mother; a mother who had cared enough to go to considerable effort to track down my location, and then a good deal more to hunt me up. Her desire to find Melissa seemed genuine to me. I couldn't understand Melissa's intense negativity toward her mother. My hand was on the phone to call Mrs. Gibson and ask her. Then, I suddenly decided that the questions I needed to ask might be the kind better asked in person. I knew all about those sort of questions. They were the ones I was always going to ask myself, tomorrow. Only tomorrow never seemed to come. Even if it ever did I probably wouldn't answer.

*   *   *

My host, Juan, was raking the gravel that served as the parking lot for the Pueblo de Bandas. A little boy with jet black hair growing wild and a runny nose followed in his wake, redistributing gravel with a smaller rake of his own. The little one, whom I assumed was Juan's son, hadn't yet mastered the smooth, neat strokes of his father. To be honest, he looked to be more hindrance than help. If Juan minded, he didn't let it show.

I had one foot inside the car when the little boy came running over to me. He ran with a funny stride, holding his legs almost stiff and shuffling his feet as though his shoes were to big for his feet. He handed me a small piece of white paper folded in half. I opened it. Large, well-formed, penciled letters said Sgt. Nichols, followed by a phone number.

Gravel crunched like broken glass beneath my feet as I walked over to Juan. He paused and leaned on the rake and looked at me with calm brown eyes. "When did he call?" I fluttered the note in the air.

Juan shrugged, "Yesterday afternoon. Five, six, somewhere in there."

"What did he want?"

"He didn't say." No expression in the voice, none in the eye. I couldn't tell if he was suppressing some emotion or if he really didn't care.

I told him thanks and trudged on back to the car. I ruffled the kid's black hair and slid in behind the wheel. The motor coughed and sputtered once, then died. I cranked it again and it fired. I turned the wheel hard and sent a shower of gravel and dust into the air. When I looked back in my rearview mirror and turned out onto Jiminez Street, Juan was smoothing out my mess with his long green rake, his brown face as calm and placid as the adobe walls that surrounded Pueblo de Bandas.

Traffic was heavy and ball-and-chain slow. After an hour I was hungry and tired of fighting the cowboys on wheels and the gawk and squawk and turned and pulled off at a mom and pop's for an early hamburger and cup of coffee. The hamburger was the size of a salad plate smothered in the lettuce, tomato, and onion. The coffee was hot, black, and strong enough to walk across the Mojave desert on its own. I was wide-eyed the rest of the way.

I made a couple of detours on the way to Gloria Gibson's. I made two phone calls and spent an hour in the public library. I wanted to find out a little more about my employer, such as why her own daughter despised her.

The first thought that had occurred to me was that maybe she had a record, had done some time. Like a lot of my theories, this one turned out to be full of holes. She had no record, at least not in New Mexico or Arizona, and the local paper didn't give her any coverage, not even in the society page. I shut down the research expedition a little after four and went in search of another cup of coffee and some rest for my tired old mud-brown eyes.

* * *

51

The day was beginning to die when I came down the last two hundred yards to the Gibson house. There was a black Lexus I hadn't seen before in the driveway. I parked on the street and sat for a moment with the windows down. Something about this case was bubbling in the back of my mind. I needed to get my thoughts in order before I talked to Gloria.

The heat of the day had begun to relent as the sun slid slowly toward the western horizon, but the air that came though the car windows was still warm enough to stick my shirt to my back within a couple of minutes. From out of sight, down the street a dog began to howl; a hot, dry thirsty howl. Neither one of us had a good handle on what was going on.

I sat very still and silent, mind open. Mouth shut. In the silence thoughts tiptoed tentatively to the edge of consciousness. There they lingered, hidden in the dark shadows of the forest of my mind. Glimpsed now and then as though they were more than apparition yet less than fact.

Ungoverned, my mind wondered like a mountain stream, each thought a water droplet. Beginning slowly as a freshet in the highlands, they grew in strength and size and numbers as they slid over the rocks of my memories and coursed down the steep slopes of yesterday until they were a blue blur rushing into an unseen valley.

A dream, that had come unbidden several times over the years, floated to the surface of the unconscious sea of my mind. It bobbed up and down there, bright and shining, inviting inspection.

This dream was always the same. It is mid-morning and a group of people are standing together on the smooth stone floor of an ancient Greek temple. I was among them. The sun shone brightly between the Doric columns and a gentle breeze teased our hair. We chatted amiably about matters of some importance, or so they seemed at that moment.

Then, even as we talked, the breeze began to stiffen and thick gray clouds began to darken the horizon. As the wind rose, I began to develop a concern for our safety. I was tempted to express my concern, but the others chatted on as before and not wanting to appear foolish I kept my thoughts to myself.

With every passing moment the sky darkened and the wind strengthened. Still my companions chatted away. It was if they were oblivious to the changes or ignorant of the potentialities.

Now the sky was black and the wind tore at our clothes. Overcoming my inhibitions I cried out a warning. No one listened. They were too busy talking, wrapped tightly in a self-centered cocoon. The wind was in my ears and my eyes and my mouth. I screamed out each of my friend's names, but the wind tore the words from my lips and silenced me.

Soon we were unable to hold our footing against the winds that grew ever strange. One by one we were forced across the stone floor, worn smooth by the passage of time. As we reached the edge of the temple those of us who were able, wrapped our arms around a column. The wind now blew so powerfully that in an instant our feet were swept away from us so that we fluttered from the columns like so many tattered flags.

Slowly, but with the certainty of eternity, the temple itself was lifted from the ground until it hovered a hundred feet above the earth, suspended in time and space. As I looked around all I could see was sky above and below and at all connecting angles. To let go of one's column seemed certain death. Yet, one at a time, my companions gradually succumbed to the wind. I watched them each float away from the temple, carried aloft by the stupendous air currents, until they were dark dots in the far-flung sky. Eventually, I was the only one left still clinging to my temple column. I told my fingers they were bands of steel. They knew better and I felt them begin to slip from the smooth marble. Always, just at the moment of release, I awoke.

Had she been with me, my grandmother could have told me the meaning of my dream. On the other hand, Cronshaw, in *Of Human Bondage*, said life had no meaning. My grandmother had died when I was twelve, and Cronshaw was only a literary device. As always, I was left alone to face the wind.

Minutes piled upon my dashboard like shiny coins, hot under the glare of the sun setting though the glass. I decided it was time for a little action and got of the car and trudged up the driveway and went and leaned on the doorbell. I could hear its distinctive dong, dong, dong, echo through the house. It was an empty sound and there was a empty feel to the whole street as if all the people had gone off and left the cars and houses and lonely dogs to fend for themselves. I counted to sixty in Spanish, then leaned on the buzzer again.

Halfway through the second set of chimes I heard footsteps and seconds later I heard the door chain being unhooked. Gloria Gibson opened the door. Even though it was only late afternoon she was wearing a big green bathrobe. It didn't go to well with her black hose and high heels. Maybe she was just getting home, or either ready to go out. Anyway, it was obvious that she wasn't expecting company.

Gloria blinked a couple of times as her eyes tried to become accustomed to the bright sunlight. Her nostrils flared as her eyes focused on who I was. "Why, Mr. Sanchez, I wasn't expecting you. I didn't forget an appointment, did I?"

She was letting me know that she didn't approve of my coming without calling first. I didn't let her know I wanted to read her face in person rather her voice over the phone when I gave her the news about Melissa. "No, we didn't have an appointment. I have some news though and since I was coming this way anyway I thought I would come by. I didn't interrupt anything, did I?"

Her painstakingly coiffured head shook no, but she stepped out on the porch and pulled the door to behind her. In her heels and stacked hair, the top of her head came mouth high on me. "What news?" she asked, showing me two rows of small, sharp teeth. A stray thought, that she looked like a shark in heels, swam across my mind.

"I found Melissa."

Her eyes widened and she stared intently toward the street. "Where is she?"

"She didn't want to come home."

A pained expression found its way to her face. "And why not?"

"That's what I thought I would ask you."

"How would I know?" Her cold, marble hard eyes read my face. "What did she say? What did she say about me?"

I tried to read her face. It was like looking at quality leather polished to a fine sheen. It told me less than nothing. "She said you were interested in money and power."

Gloria Gibson shrugged slim shoulders. "Aren't we all, at least to some degree, Mr. Sanchez?"

I shrugged back. "She gave me this impression that those things mean a lot to you." There was some kind of low shuffling noise emanating from deep inside the house. It sounded as though it was coming closer to the front door. Unconsciously I paused; Gloria read my eyes and followed their line of vision to the house. Out of the corner of my eye I could see her watching me. I knew what she was going to say before she said it.

"Go on," she urged, "what else did she say?"

I dragged my attention back to the conversation. "She said she was your little money maker."

Her eyes blinked once, down deep, but she kept her voice calm and controlled. "I wonder what in the world she meant by that?" She smiled as though she found the question quaintly perplexing and leaned back with exaggerated casualness against the bright red front door. I wondered if she was suddenly tired, or if it was an unconscious response to the shuffling noise that crept ever closer to the door.

"I don't know. She didn't say too much more than that, except that I should ask you." I jerked my head toward the house. "Do you need to see about that?"

"What? Oh, that noise; its nothing, just my old dog, Ingrid. She moves rather slowly these days. I am afraid I am going to have to put her down before long." She gave me a smile that didn't drift north of her lips. "Where did you say my daughter was, Mr. Sanchez?"

"I didn't, and you can drop the mister." There was something about the woman I didn't like and I could feel the strain of dealing with such feelings toward my employer pressing down like a load of bricks on my shoulders. At last I shrugged, but that weight didn't go off my back. "Sorry, it's been a long day. Melissa was at a rather luxurious ranch a few miles outside of Santa Fe. As far as I could tell, she was there of her own free will and didn't seem to be having too bad a time. I didn't get much of a chance to talk with her, but what little conversation we had made it very clear that she didn't want anything to do with you. What's the problem, Mrs. Gibson?"

It was her turn to shrug. "Teenagers in general can be difficult to deal with, Mr. Sanchez; teenage girls can be downright impossible."

"What did she mean by the money maker comment?"

She answered me obliquely. "All relationships have their rough spots. Communication, for the last several months, has been that problem area for Melissa and me. We hadn't been talking much anyway, and when we did it wasn't productive. I thought that by giving her some time and space it might get better. Obviously I was wrong."

"How does that explain the money maker language?"

"It doesn't, except that I'm saying that the two of us drifted a little bit apart and settled on different wave lengths. So I don't really know what meaning she was ascribing to those words. She is my daughter and I'm worried about her. Why didn't you make her come home?" The last sentence was more accusation than question.

"That wasn't my job. Besides she didn't want to. I was hired to find her and I did. Melissa is very much alive and well, and very clear about her intention to keep her distance from you. My advice, Mrs. Gibson, is to leave her alone for a while. Teenagers change from one day to the next. A few weeks, a month from now, she may wake up one morning and decide to come home."

A slim hand slid slowly across my left shoulder. "Take me to her, Mr. Sanchez."

"No, that wasn't part of our deal." I shrugged the hand off. The woman gave me the creeps. I didn't want her touching me.

"I can simply hire somebody else," she said. There was steel in the voice and ice in the eyes.

"So do it." I gave her my tired old coyote smile and trudged down the driveway. Halfway to the car I could still hear the shuffling inside. That was one large dog.

CHAPTER 15

The sun was a wet splotch of yellow on the eastern horizon; a sunny side up egg splattered against the bright blue east sky. A few clouds, too small and ineffectual to diminish the morning hung low against the hills. It was the first time I had been outside my adobe walls in two days and I moved unsteadily across the rocky ground like a leg weary fighter in the thirteenth round. By the time I reached the narrow path that twisted and turned its way up my hill I had the kinks out and was moving at a steady, comfortable pace. The chill of dawn was wearing off rapidly and I could feel the sweat forming in small pools under my arms.

I was out of breath by the time I got to the hilltop. In the thin clear air I could hear myself panting faintly like an old dog who can no longer run with the pack. Vegetation was sparse here. A few tufts of what I called prairie grass grew scattered here and there, as though the seeds had been sown by a playful child. A single prickly pear curled low and snug beneath the shelter of one of the many outcroppings of rock. The rocks were numerous here, and came in so many shapes and sizes, textures, thickness, and hues that I wished I had paid more attention to my Geology teacher at Weber State. However, Norman Clark had also been the golf coach, and it was much more interesting at the time, and better for my grade point average, to get him off geology and talking about the latest golf match in which his team had managed to snatch defeat from the jaws of victory. His teams were quite bad during my years there, so awful in fact that I had tried out for the squad. My lack of ability to keep my drives even close to landing in the fairway has doomed my attempt almost from the start.

I carefully picked my way over to a large mottled gray and black ledge that jutted out from the crest like a flying buttress. Here on the top of the ridge the ground was covered with a frosting of small loose stones, many smooth and slick. It was as though some giant had decorated the peak like the top of some wonderful, monstrous birthday cake, using the small stones as little candy pieces.

Easing my way out to the end of the ledge I could see a narrow, elongated valley stretched before me. It was much like my valley on the other side of the mountains, except that the terrain was less steep, and given more to sudden small mounds of earth separated by quick, nasty dark crevices that littered the hillside like foreboding pits of destruction. The shadows created by the mounds and the darkness of the crevices gave the slope an evil appearance, as though it were the terrain of some dark and deadly people.

Midway down the slope was a ring of trees. The trees were a mixed lot, mostly mesquite, with a few oak, spruce, and even a small cottonwood thrown in for contrast. This woody ring was no more than twenty yards across at its widest point and shrunk in several places to a single tree. It ran from the far right of my field of vision across the hill until it disappeared into the shadows of a quintet of giant boulders that formed the boundary of my view to the left. The tree ring appeared to be growing here for no particular reason. There was no visible stream, and the ground beneath the branches looked no more promising than that of its neighbors to the north or south. The green leaves and dark brown trunks and limbs combined to give the copse an aura of magic.

Far below, on the valley floor, was the remains of an old working ranch. The roofs of a couple of the out buildings had fallen in, and one of the wide front doors of the faded red barn swung to and fro on rusty hinges. Several sections of the wooden fence that had formed the corral were down, and tumbleweeds had blown into the four corners. From my perch, however, the old stone house looked solid, except for a tall rock-and-mortar chimney on the north end that was falling in on itself.

It was my understanding that the old farmhouse was on the reservation and, therefore, not occupied. However, the dirt around the front of the house looked to be beaten smooth, and my eye could follow a clearly defined path that wormed its way through the weeds and boulders until it disappeared in a small oak grove. Somebody was certainly using it on a regular basis. I wondered whose feet traveled the path.

I wondered enough to pick my way down a half lost path that moved sporadically and spasmodically in long, curving loops down the hillside. A dead cedar was across it in one place, and it disappeared completely in a couple more. When it vanished, I had to chart my own course across the uneven ground. Once, a reddish brown squirrel skillfully worked his way around the trunk of an ancient oak. I saw several small lizards and the rear end of a retreating green snake. High above me, a black wedge in a cobalt blue sky, a hawk soared against filmy white clouds.

Forty minutes after I started down the slope, I was hot, tired, thirsty, and finally on level ground. A gap-toothed wooden plank fence hinted at a separation of land masses. A sun bleached cow's skull impaled on the top of a corner fence post marked someone's territory or twisted sense of humor. I stepped through one of the gaps in the fence and crossed the final twenty yards of nearly bare ground to the house.

The stones were still solid, a quiet testimony to their strength and endurance and the skill of the builder. The windows were another story. Well over half the panes were smashed out entirely, and most of the remainder were chipped or cracked. The front door was firmly shut, but the rear door hung ajar a good six inches. From the outside the cabin looked dark, dusty, and uninviting. I could see a cane-backed chair with a broken leg, a small table with arthritis, and an empty bottle of Jack Daniels. There was a ragged blue and green checked blanket in one corner along with a stack of magazines without covers, and yellowing newspapers. I pushed the back door open another four inches and squeezed inside.

*　　*　　*

Powdery dust lay like a new snow on the floorboards and windowsills. There were tracks in this strange gray snow; all sorts of tracks. I could see cat tracks, dog tracks, even bird tracks. There were wild animal tracks I couldn't identify and man-made tracks I could. At least two styles, and maybe three sizes, of running or basketball shoes had been here. They went with the empty Pringles and Bud cans piled in one corner. Somebody who had been here had a sweet tooth as evidenced by the crumbled brown Snickers' wrappers. Someone drank Diet Coke, and someone smoked Camels. There was a strong, sweet, musty odor to the room, as if an earlier visitor had smoked something even more lethal.

I wandered through the empty cabin. It wasn't much, one good sized bedroom, a primitive kitchen with a tall narrow pantry, the cluttered living room, and a small storage room full of leftover odds and ends. A rusty shovel with a broken handle, a broom with only two inches of straw left, a pile of *Look* magazines, an art painting of Lake Mead that was ripped in the upper right corner, a few old pots and pans, a gooseneck lamp patched together with electrical tape, a half dozen paperbacked versions of the classics, some pint jars full of an unidentifiable reddish brown liquid, empty sixteen gauge shotgun shells, a blue marble, a 1965 calendar turned to March, and a forty-five vinyl Johnny Cash record. A pathetic collection of livability, not so very unlike one I had on the other side of the mountain.

The most interesting thing I found was a stained, tattered mattress with the stuffing oozing out. It was in the bedroom pushed up against the wall under a window that still had three of the four panes of glass. A half dozen cigarette butts resided in a pie pan ashtray. A used rubber and a empty tube of lipstick, Spring Peach was the designated color, kept them company. A badly worn, but genuine, Navajo blanket lay haphazardly across the mattress.

I knelt down on the mattress and looked out the window. The view through the dusty glass was surprisingly good. A modest cottonwood was framed in the center with a half dozen small pines growing up to the left. Years ago someone had planted a rose bush to the right of the tree, and I could see pink buds on the branches. A small stream trickled down from a distant hillside and wended its way through the ground in back of the cottonwood. Grass grew bravely along its edges, and I could see a small, well-shaped, brown bird tiptoeing through the dampness along the edge of the cut the stream had made in the earth over the course of the years.

It was the most verdant site I had seen in my wanderings, and a cool breeze fluttered the leaves of the cottonwood. I liked the darkened dusty house with its stained mattress and collection of used cans. My legs were tired from my wanderings, so I lay down on the lumpy mattress. I pulled the blanket up to me, wadded it into a rectangular shape, and stuck it under my head for a pillow. I closed my eyes. I could smell dust and dirt, and the faint odor of human sweat and perfume. The brown bird, or its mate, began to sing. The wind blew in through the missing window pane and kissed my cheek.

*   *   *

I dreamed I was on a slow moving train. The tracks wound in ever tightening spirals around a mountain so tall that the crest disappeared into cottony clouds. If I looked out the window of my car, I could see for hundreds of feet down into a rock strewn gorge. A tiny blue vein of a river trickled across the floor of the gorge. I had a strange certainty inside me that it was a view previously seen only by Indians and eagles.

A brown-haired girl in a red dress sat on the seat beside me. Two men sat on the leather seat on the other side of the car. However, they were merely dim shadows of themselves. It was as if the cloud had drifted down from the mountain peak and shrouded them in secrecy. Their faces were ghostly blanks, their voices faint murmurs.

The girl and I were arguing. She was urging me to go back to where I had begun my journey. She kept speaking of unfinished business. It was hot in the compartment from the sunlight pouring through the long plate glass windows and I was tired of arguing with her. She was a difficult sort, sharp tongued, persistent, and given to elaborating on her points at great length. The most difficult thing about her, however, was her hair. It hung thick and long like a soft brown curtain that hid her face from view. I sensed, with a certainty I could not explain, that she had a very lovely face. That only made it doubly frustrating that I wasn't able to see beyond the curtain of brown.

So the train chugged upwards, I began to work up a fixation about seeing that face. The longer we argued, the more sharp her remarks, the more determined I became to see it. In my preoccupation and frustration with her hair and face, I began to lose track of the argument. The point of contention no longer seemed worthy of discussion. I sensed that the two men across the car were enjoying my discomfort. Their presence, however, no longer mattered. Maddened by the long, mahogany brown hair that hid her face, I suddenly stretched out my hand to pull it aside.

I awoke with my right hand grasping at empty air. It took me several seconds to pull my wits back about me and remember where I was. Sweat trickled down the back of my neck. A fly droned solemnly against one of the panes of glass in the window above my head. The air in the cabin was hot and still. I wiped the dampness from my forehead and sat up on the mattress with the broken back. In the movies I would have reached in my flannel shirt pocket and pulled out a pack of cigarettes, non-filter, non-menthol. This wasn't the movies and I didn't smoke. I did want badly a cup of coffee, but that wasn't in the cards, so I turned and looked out the window, watched the world go by, buried one more day.

*   *   *

The view from the window was truly lovely, certainly more verdant and lush than anything on my side of the mountain. A jay came swooping in from the west and landed on a slender branch near the top of a mesquite tree and sat there swinging to and fro. Sunlight reached the ground, filtered by the leaves and branches, dappling the grass here and there, spotlighting odd shapes and patterns as if they had been chosen by lottery. Picturesque is the way most magazine writers would have described the scene, and they would have been correct. Yet, I preferred my lonely, rocky, brown slice of life. My sunbaked, windswept, not forgotten adobe was far more me than this postcard picture of Eden.

The jay swang and sang to himself for some time. If he were waiting on his mate, he was waiting in vain. Eventually tiring of his flimsy perch, he flapped his wings and fluttered to the ground, disappearing in seconds in the tall shadowy grasses that grew along the bank of the stream. The gentle breeze had begun to blow more steadily, and it ruffled the tops of the grasses so that I was unable to follow the path of the bird.

My mind was clouded with random thoughts, and yet strangely benumbed, as if the sheer number of images had overwhelmed that portion of the mind designed to channel them into coherent structures. I sat on the mattress for a long time, long enough to watch the shadows change as the sun made its march, long enough to feel the dryness spread across my throat, long enough to see the girl come through the tall grass that grew in the flats of the curve the water had carved.

When the grass first rippled with her coming, I thought it was the wind, then a wild animal—a coyote or a muledeer. It was only when she was within a dozen steps of the water that I saw what she was. Even then, I didn't recognize her at first. She looked older from a distance, moving with a mature, certain stride that indicated she knew where she was going and exactly how to get there. It was only when she looked up at my window, just after she had jumped the stream at its narrowest point, that I saw she was the soul stealer. Her full mouth, that was nearly the width of the lower part of her heart-shaped face, and the deep rich brown eyes, set too far apart for the narrowness of her skull, revealed her identity.

My instinct was to rouse myself from the strange stupor that had embraced me since I'd entered the bedroom, but my prideful ego refused to allow me to run from a slender girl of mixed blood who appeared to be unarmed and not a day over eighteen. In the back of my mind, a little voice whispered that pride goeth before the fall.

CHAPTER 16

Her steps were light and quick as she moved across the packed earth in front of the door. She moved with a certain sureness that told me she had been this way before. There was a brief pause, only a second or two, at the threshold before I heard the door squeak on its hinges.

The old floorboards protested to themselves in the quiet of the early afternoon. Footsteps moved sporadically through the kitchen and down the hall, pausing every thirty seconds or so as if she were looking out a window. She was humming, very softly, to herself. It was a slow, melodic tune. I didn't recognize it.

I put my back up against the wall under the window and waited for her. I felt vulnerable and exposed, not afraid exactly, although I certainly didn't relish seeing her slight figure appear in my doorway.

Her shadow came first, a soft, mushy, feeble shadow barely formed by such poor light as had penetrated the short, narrow hall. Just outside my door the shadow paused, as if the form sensed my presence. Perhaps, just below the surface of her conscious senses, she had picked up my odor. If she felt fear she choked it down and came on, sticking her head boldly around the corner as if she owned the place.

Her mahogany eyes locked onto mine and we stared unsmiling into each other's eyes. The silence lengthened and thickened between us as if it were a new life form creating its own image.

She stood like a carved slab of ivory, framed by the wooden rectangle where the door had once hung. Nothing about her moved, except that her thin chest rose and fell slowly under her faded red and green flannel shirt. Now and then, when the light was just right, I caught sight of the flecks of gold that flashed in the pupils of her eyes. Her wide lips were slightly parted, and I could have counted her white, even teeth. Her mouth and eyes were both so oversized and widespread in her small heart-shaped face that they seemed to be consuming her from the inside.

Seconds ticked into minutes in the clock inside my head. The whole world seemed to have gone into slow motion, so that the time capsules formed like large elongated drops of water at the edge of the spout before falling slowly into a dark abyss below. The silence was so complete that I could hear my breath rasp in my throat, and my heart thump in my chest. The ends of my fingers felt cold, and a nerve in my left leg jumped of its own accord.

When she came across the room it was with slow, measured steps—stalking steps—each foot planted carefully before she raised the other. The hairs on the back of my neck bristled.

Two feet away from me she stopped and squatted back on her heels until her eyes were level with mine. Golden flecks swam in twin, murky, mahogany pools. Burnished copper skin was drawn tight across cheekbones so prominent that they threatened to slice through the flesh. Her wide mouth opened slowly as she inclined her head toward me. Her breath smelled faintly of peppermint. A long brown ponytail swung freely at the back of her finely molded skull.

"Who are you?" She breathed, rather than spoke, the question. Her voice was deep for one so young, rumbling around somewhere in the bowels of her throat.

"The name is Sanchez."

"I know your name," she hissed back as quickly as a striking rattlesnake. "You live on the far side of the mountain in the old Baxter place. You drive a 1982 Jeep Cherokee, and have no visible means of support. You have been gone for a week, you drink Maxwell House coffee, and your subscription to National Geographic expires in August."

"So you break into houses as well as stare at them from the outside."

"You should lock your door, old man."

"I have nothing anybody would want to steal."

"I know. I ate your last two chocolate chip cookies. They were getting awfully dry. I hope you don't mind." There were strangely wonderful golden lights in her eyes. I had the feeling that inside she was laughing at me, though her lips didn't move.

"Do you get everything you want?" I was furious and fascinated by her all in the same instant.

"As long as I don't want too much." This time her lips did curl up in a cruel self-parody of a smile.

I had a sense that the girl was playing at something far beyond the word game in which we were engaged. I tried to get at the underlying significance. "And what do you want?"

She leaned forward until she invaded my personal space. I could feel her warm breath on my cheeks. Her little pink tongue pushed its way along the outside of her upper row of snow white teeth. She looked into my eyes for a very long moment. I caught myself holding my breath and expelled it slowly like air seeping from a pin prick in a balloon.

She came even closer, so close her features were almost blurred. Our lips couldn't have been more than an inch apart. "What if I want you, old white man who lives in the crazy crumbling purple adobe?"

This creature owned me. I could feel my heart flutter like a butterfly on cocaine. There was a sickness in my soul. She knew too much, too fast. She was a skinwalker, a witch, a fallen angel from hell. I couldn't speak; I didn't trust my voice. A stray thought slid across my mind that if I broke under her spell I would die. I made my eyes stone, and gave her the silent treatment.

She took it for a minute, rocking back and forth on her heels, before she spoke.

"What's the matter, old man? You afraid of a young mestizo girl? Come on, talk to me. I won't bite." She punctuated the sentence with a smile that featured the vast majority of her teeth.

"What are you?" There was a lump as hard as a rock, and as big as a baseball in my throat.

"I'm your worst nightmare." There was a satanic snarl in her voice, but her eyes were laughing at me.

"You're teenage trouble on two legs. Why don't you go away and leave me alone."

"Maybe this is my house."

"Yeah, and maybe I'm Santa Claus." I thought about her remark for a minute, then asked, "Who does own this place?"

"I do," she laughed. She looked out from under her long eyelashes to see if I was paying attention. Satisfied that I was, she added, "Just kidding. I really don't know who owns it." She wrinkled her nose at the dirty floor and grimy walls. "Looks like it hasn't been lived in for years. My friends and I discovered it late last summer and I thought about it all winter. The rest of them didn't like it, but I did. Since it's abandoned and we found it, I figure it belongs to us. I sort of inherited it when the rest of them didn't want to come back." Her eyes were wide open, but she wasn't seeing anything in the room. She was miles away.

"Why didn't they like it?"

Her white teeth made indentations in her upper lip. "They think it's just an old rundown barn of a building. A place to come to make out, smoke, and dance. You know, have a party. It's a long way from the Pueblo, though. There are lots of places just as good for that a whole lot closer."

"How far away is it?"

Her eyes retreated back into the room and focused on me. "Two miles. No, more. Three."

"You walked all that way?"

"Sure. I do it a couple times a week when the weather's good."

"You must really like it."

"Oh, I do," she answered eagerly. "I think it's the neatest old house. There is so much more room here than I'm used to, and privacy. Every room has a door, and two of them even lock." Her lips formed a smile of genuine pleasure. "I know. I've tried them. But do you know what I like best of all?"

I shook my head. "No."

"The memories."

"What memories? Did you live here before?"

She laughed at me a little, gently. "No, silly. The memories of the people that lived here before. At least some of them were named Henderson. I found an old letter in one of the bedrooms."

"How can you know about someone else's memories?"

Her smile said she knew a secret. "I can feel them, sense them. I know it sounds crazy, but it's true. It's like they're here, hiding in the walls, and they only come out when I'm alone and it's real quiet. Sometimes they're such happy memories that I feel warm all over. Other times," she shrugged and shivered a little. Her pink tongue traced the outline of her lips, and she opened her eyes extra wide and gave me a fleeting little smile.

I sat very silent and still as she rose and walked stiff legged over to the window, where she stood as straight as a flag pole, with her back to me. It was so quiet in the old house that I could hear the boards pop and creak as they expanded to meet the sun. I waited for a long time, looking at her straight, slim back, and waiting for the memories.

She never turned to look at me and no memories visited me. Just before three, I got up and started back to my adobe, leaving her alone with the old house and the hot and cold running memories. About halfway to the crest of the hill, I realized I didn't even know her name.

CHAPTER 17

He was the color of dried sage, and no more than six inches long from the point of his nose to the tip of his slender tail. He had just poked his head out of a dark crevice midway up the rock that adjoined the one I had my back against. The sun was bright and hot and unencumbered by clouds. It beat down on us without mercy. It was only ten o'clock in the morning and already the temperature had to be well into the eighties.

Five hundred feet below me was the valley, a round bowl sparsely covered with golden bush and yucca. Here and there, saguaro cactus stood like soldiers in the midst of field maneuvers. A small trail of packed earth snaked its way from south to north across the canyon floor. High above even my perch, a wedge-shaped speck circled lazily, riding the thermals in ever widening orbits as it searched for a meal.

It was two days since I'd made my trek to the abandoned ranchhouse. I hadn't set foot outside of my adobe between then and this morning. The walls had finally started to close in on me and I swallowed the last of the strong, better mixture of fear and confusion that had clung to my throat for forty-eight hours.

Melissa Gibson had been on my mind for the last twenty-four. The whole situation bothered me. The gun-toting guards, her refusal to leave, the obvious loathing of her mother, that leather-skinned lady of iron, herself; nothing rang true. Gloria Gibson didn't bother me. I didn't like her, wouldn't trust her. I had taken her money and found her wayward daughter. I wouldn't do it again, not for double the price.

The girl, however, was a problem.

She worried me, or rather I worried about her. There was an intensity about her passionate refusal that was more than teenage angst. It was raw, undiluted hatred. Melissa and her mother had come to a parting of the ways and the gap between then seemed canyonesque.

It wasn't that I wanted to bring them together. I sensed that it wasn't the time or place and that perhaps there never would be. It was more that the girl was a woman in the making, and something deep in my gut told me she was in the hands of the wrong sculptor.

It wasn't my business and it wasn't my nature to stick my nose in where it had no business, but a restlessness had swallowed my soul. A restlessness as strong and intense as the winds that whistled among the massive boulders hundreds of feet above the round canyon floor. I could feel the restless forces against my cheek and deep in my soul. I blinked at the little lizard and he blinked his golden eyes open and shut in return. Above us, the bird soared higher and wider, circling over his whole world. The rock was oven hot to the touch. My shirt was stuck to my back and rivulets of sweat ran down my side and spine. I rose slowly on weak and trembling legs and took the first steps back to my adobe, and Melissa Gibson.

*   *   *

Santa Fe by moonlight is a glorious sight. I rolled in from the north on a back road the locals referred to as the old mountain highway, under a full moon bright enough to read the Albuquerque Journal by. I could have turned off my headlights and drifted along in the shining silver pathway. In my younger and bolder days, I probably would have done so. A stray thought filtered across my mind that I was really lucky to have lived so long.

Traffic was light even as I approached the outskirts of this rose of New Mexico. It was after midnight, and most of the locals and virtually all of the tourists had gone to ground for the night. A state trooper flew by me headed south, and I sailed by a local cop sitting in a black and white half hidden in the shadows of the old Greyhound station. In my college days I had caught a bus or two from there. Nobody caught one now; they had boarded the depot up about 1983. The cop was asleep or didn't have his radar on; I was doing fifty-seven in a forty-five mile per hour zone.

I tapped the brakes a couple of times as I approached downtown. A smattering of bars and restaurants still gave off light and evidence of life, but most of the shops were closed and dark. I swung wide at the corner of State and Jefferson in order to miss a tall, thin white man in a "Bulls" cap meandering drunkenly off the sidewalk and out into the street. Down by the La Fonda, a beefy guy who looked like Ned Beatty on steroids pulled up alongside in a Ferrari and gave me an evil look. I wasn't who he was looking for, and he revved up his engine and left me in his wake.

I caught every light right but had to come to a complete stop to let a Taurus wagon from Tennessee pull into the Pueblo Bonito. The weatherman on the radio promised fair skies and a warmer tomorrow. So had my first wife.

A bright yellow bulb burned above the porch that jutted out from the office of the Pueblo de Bandas. There were three cars and two pickups parked in the gravel lot. It was 12:52 according to my watch. I pulled off the street, eased the Cherokee to a stop, and turned the key. For a pair of minutes I sat with my arms on the wheel, letting the waves of tiredness wash over me, and listened to the pop and ping of the engine as it cooled in the night air. A squadron of moths flung themselves violently against the yellow bug light above the wooden planks of the porch. It was five minutes before one when I opened my door and went to join them.

The floorboards groaned in protest under my weight and the screen door squeaked raucously on its hinges as it swung open. I could feel tiredness rubbing at the back of my neck as I stepped into the small office. The room might have been eight by ten and most of it was taken up by a large, old fashioned, high topped counter with a cash register on the left hand side and a two-tiered rack of mail slots on the wall behind. Only two slots had any mail in them, and all the keys were there except for four. A key dangled on a beaded chain from the hook in front of number fourteen.

There was nobody behind the counter, and I listened for a moment to try and hear them stirring behind one of the twin doors set in the back wall. All I heard was the rise and fall of a police siren in the distance moving away and the metronomic tick-tock of the ancient Regulator clock that hung on the windowless walls to my right. My dad still had the same brand of clock that had hung in his office during his first superintendency at Pineville, Missouri.

I gave the desk clerk twenty seconds to come out. When he didn't, I tapped the bell on the counter twice. Its sharp ring split the silence of the stale night air. In a few seconds I fancied that I could hear some rustling behind door number two, and sure enough the door to my right swung open revealing first a blob of empty hole of nothingness and then a disheveled Juan simultaneously rubbing the sleep from his eyes and tugging at his fallen suspenders.

Just short of the counter, he recognized me and managed a wan smile. "Señor Sanchez, it is good to see you again so soon. I hadn't counted on such a quick return visit."

I answered the question hiding behind the words. "Duty calls. Is number fourteen still available?"

He made a show of turning and making sure the key was still there. Facing me again, he responded gravely that it was.

"Let me have it then."

"For how many night?"

I laid three worn pictures of Andrew Jackson on the table. "I'm not sure exactly how long I'll be in town this time. Will this cover me for three nights?"

"*Sí*, Señor." He gave me a smile with more wattage and spun the register around with a flourish. "Sign here, please," he said, marking the line with a slim blue Parker fountain pen.

"Sorry to get you up this late," I said by way of an apology.

"Never too late for a good customer. Besides, with a face like mine, who needs beauty rest?" He smiled at his own self-parody. He was missing a molar or two and the teeth remaining were replete with cavities, but his smile was genuine and his sleepy brown eyes twinkled in the light of the old owl's head lamp that jutted up from the far left quadrant of the counter.

I took the key out of his extended hand and flashed him my best "good night" and "thank you" combination smile. I went and got my battered Samsonite and raggedy gym bag out of the Cherokee and trudged across the gravel to number fourteen.

A trio of moths fluttered half-heartedly at the bug light that beamed above my door. I tended to agree with them; it was too late for any extreme exertions. Tiredness had been lapping at my heels since I'd hit town. Now it rose up and swept over me like a tsunami. I kicked the door shut behind me and flung my bags in a corner, then stretched out on the swaybacked double bed like I owned it. The waves lapped at the base of my brain and then it was all darkness, a deep well from which there was no escape. An image of my mother floated briefly into my remaining consciousness, washing out of the past. She had been gone for thirty years. The mind was a strong and terrible force. The world of random thoughts and haphazard dreams was beyond my comprehension. I started to raise my head and turn over, but, at that moment, it seemed too much trouble.

*   *   *

Sunlight streamed across my face like hot smoke. For a moment I wasn't sure where I was, then I wasn't sure why. I figured out an answer to the first question but not the second. My body protested that it wasn't twenty-one anymore, but I made it get up anyway.

I dug a worn pair of Asics, some reasonably clean socks, running shorts, and my Save The Whales T-shirt out of my gym bag and put them on. I stumbled blinking into the bright sunshine of a New Mexico morning and started putting one foot in front of the other. My body grumbled and fumed all the way to the Copper Canyon road before it loosened up and the feet and yards began to flow. I ran past school kids riding their bikes to Math and English, past mothers pushing baby carriages, and old winos still sleeping off the night before in the shade of the mesquite that lined the concrete drainage ditches. The birds were out in force, singing of their enjoyment of the morning, and a bushy-tailed gray squirrel nearly pulled out in front of me.

My legs found some long forgotten freshness, and I ran like I was sixteen again. In twenty minutes I felt like I belonged on the Olympics team. In thirty, I turned and headed back for a shower and shave. I wanted to go looking for trouble before it came hunting for me.

CHAPTER 18

It looked like the house party from hell. The desert's longest running sex, drugs, and fun club was looking a bit frazzled, frayed at the ends you might say. The guard at the front I didn't recognize. The one at the back was a holdover from my previous visit. Not that it mattered, neither one could have caught his own shadow. They were both half asleep in the late afternoon sunshine. Another hour, and darkness would begin its nocturnal creep across the arid landscape.

I was just thirty yards short of the drive that circled in front of the low-slung ranch on a boulder strewn rise in the land. I was wedged in between a large gray boulder and a saguaro cactus. Anybody looking this way from the house would get an eyeful of sun and figure me for a skinny boulder or a misshapen cactus. Occupying the high ground gave me a bird's eye view into the compound.

Since I had been there last, a certain degree of deterioration had set in. Empty beer cans and whiskey bottles were scattered about the yard and around the pool's edge. A dozen or so Budweiser cans lined up single file on a diving board tilting forty degrees to starboard. They looked like pirate captives about to walk the plank.

Discarded T-shirts and bikini tops littered the landscape. An occasional magazine or romance novel lay unattended by an empty deck chair. Residing at the bottom of the shallow end of the pool was a deck chair that had had one too many. A big-chested blonde lay on her back, passed out and oblivious to the sun that was turning her bare breasts a startling shade of hot pink. A skinny man with a face full of dried blood lay on his left side near the edge of the low stone fence that separated the pool from the blacktop parking area at the rear of the house. I had watched him with some degree of closeness for the past half hour. He hadn't moved.

A blue version of last year's Mustang sat in the middle of the back parking area with both doors wide open. A small dog yapped with aggravating frequency from inside the house. Fortunately, someone had Boyz To Men turned up loudly enough to drown out most of his sorrows. Once, I heard a loud peal of feminine laughter followed by the slamming of a door.

Shadows had crept across the enclosed yard of sand, golden bush, and yucca when the silver phone sitting on the black wrought iron table near the southern edge of the pool began ringing. No one bothered to answer it. I began to count the rings and got to twenty-five before I gave up. It took the caller another couple of minutes to call it quits, but the ringing eventually stopped.

I waited until the shadows had crept completely across the yard and merged with the darkness that had slid silently in behind me. Hours of waiting in the rocky terrain had given me an opportunity to fix a path in my mind, and I followed the memory among the brittlebrush and loose stones.

No one challenged me as I eased through the thickening dark. Pool lights and the yellow bug light over the back door illuminated the backyard. Once inside the circle of lights, I walked across the balance of the grounds as though I owned it. I slowed as my shoes scuffed along the concrete patio. I eased my way into an elongated shadow cast by a furled pool umbrella and rested my cheek against the bricks directly below the kitchen window. They were still warm.

The murmurs of voices on the other side of the bricks blended with the babbling of an unseen television set playing somewhere off to my right. None of the voices was clear enough for me to distinguish any words. I straightened up slowly until I was on my tiptoes. At this height I could just see over the kitchen windowsill.

The kitchen looked like the aftermath of Spring Break at Daytona Beach. Dirty glasses, plates, and utensils filled the sink to overflowing and staggered drunkenly along the black and white Formica counter. A half eaten pizza was slowly congealing in its cardboard box. A double handful of abandoned beer cans stood guard over a half empty bottle of Chablis.

On the far side of the kitchen, the cream colored wall was broached by an arch. Lounging up against the left side of the arch was a tall, thin man in a light blue golf shirt. He didn't look much like a golfer to me, at least from the rear, which was all I could see. His black hair was thin and scraggly. He wore it long, letting it ride far down his neck, long enough to obscure his shirt collar. It shone as though coated with grease. His arms were thin and pale, as if he spent very little time in the desert sunshine. The bones of his thin legs threatened to push through the seat of his tan slacks. The only thing that kept him from looking like a total wimp was the nasty little .38 special dangling from the leather holster that hung around his neck and under his left shoulder.

Beyond Thin and Nasty was another room. I could see a flickering television, a pair of half-filled bookshelves and what looked like a real Georgia O'Keefe on the wall. A pair of running shoes, attached to feet that extended out of my view, poked out from behind the wall that separated the kitchen from the den. The shoes looked at least three sizes too big for Melissa.

I came down off my toes and began easing my way around to my left. That was the long end of the house, and back on the hill I had counted at least three windows that were set lower in the brick than the one in the kitchen. I figured that bedrooms lay behind them.

Moving carefully among the clutter and cacti that competed for space in the backyard, I slid alongside the house, making sure I kept close to the wall and well in the shadows. I hadn't seen any sign of movement from the guard in the back. However, I had been concentrating on what was inside the house and the outside factors could have changed with the coming of the dark.

* * *

Beyond the last window lay only an empty bedroom. By the light of the overhead I could see an unmade bed, a long narrow dresser, and a tall chest of drawers. The top of the chest of drawers was a mare's nest set of open cosmetic cases, used Kleenex, and a battery of lipstick tubes—ammunition for all invasions.

I moved on down the side of the house, going along in a low crouch. The windows here were only breast high, and I didn't want some inquisitive spirit to get a good look at me. I eased my way to the second window and slowly raised my head.

Beyond the glass was a bathroom, occupied. A man about my height with thick, jet black hair stood before the toilet. His urine ran in a steady stream as he swayed slightly from side to side as though he were responding to music only he could hear. His eyes were closed and his mouth hung half open. I ducked down before he reversed their status.

The third room was darker than the other two, lighted only by a flickering television. In the dimness, it took me a few seconds to bring the room's contents into focus.

There were curtains on the window. However, they were gapped at least six inches in the middle, and I had a decent view of the center two thirds of the room.

A large brass bed occupied the bulk of the space. The cover on it was neatly and smoothly spread. A pair of slim brown legs lounged atop the bedspread. I maneuvered further to my left so I would have a better line of sight. I needed to see to whom the legs belonged.

I should have gone to Vegas; my luck was running good. Both legs belonged to Melissa. She was lying on her back, her head propped up by two giant pillows, staring at the television. I couldn't be certain because of the dim lighting, but she didn't seem to be very intent on the action taking place on the tube. Her expression somehow left me with the distinct impression that her focus was inward. I could see that her bedroom door, which I assumed opened into a hallway of some sort, was closed. There was a single easy chair and small writing table to accompany the standard chest and dresser. Her closet door was tightly closed and the top of the chest and dresser were as empty as a lunar landscape. Melissa wasn't leaving much of herself in the room.

I pulled a quarter out of my pocket and rapped lightly on the window. The brown legs didn't move. I rapped again, three staccato beats. This time the legs swung over my side of the bed. I watched them cross the carpeted floor slowly and warily as if they were afraid.

When the legs reached the window, they stopped and bent at the knees. Melissa's face came down through the darkness and stared at me through the glass. In the murky light, she was out of focus and strangely disfigured. I watched her face change from wondering about who was out there, to knowing it was a man, to recognizing me. Ultimately she gave me a look that was a tincture of disgust and fear. I wondered why she was afraid of me.

"Open the window," I whispered.

She hesitated, then shook her head no.

"Melissa, open up. I need to talk to you."

The fine brown legs straightened up and the head disappeared above my line of sight. I was afraid I was losing her. In a couple of seconds, however, I heard the window rattle in its frame as it slid open about six inches.

"What do you want?"

"I want to talk to you for a few minutes. You never called or came by my motel."

"So?" She made the single syllable mean that she was bored and I was stupid. Perhaps she was right on both counts.

"So, I got to worrying about you. The way you seemed to feel about your mother got me to wondering. If things aren't good between you two at home, well, perhaps there might be other places that would be better than this party. Seems to me as though it is well past its prime."

Her face swam back down out of the void of darkness. She pressed her nose against the screen. I leaned in closer. From this shortened distance, her lips looked swollen and one of her eyes was surrounded by a yellowish circle of flesh.

"Somebody been beating you?"

"What happened to me is my business and none of yours."

"I'm making it mine." Our mouths were less than an inch apart, separated only by a thin wire screen and a great gulf of misunderstanding. The conversation seemed to be going nowhere, except maybe around in ever

74

tightening circles like a dog chasing its tail. I tightened the circles another turn. "Looks like somebody had better be looking after you."

She jerked her had back in an angry response. "I can take care of myself," she hissed.

"What about the busted lip and the black eye?"

"What about them?"

"They didn't just happen. Somebody has been doing a number on your face. You're young and pretty now, but let a few more fists bang up against your head and you won't be pretty anymore, and you may not live to be old."

She shrugged. In the ensuing quiet I could hear distant shouts over the babbling murmurs of the television. They didn't sound particularly like shouts of anger or alarm, they just sounded like shouts.

Melissa closed her eyes for a moment. I looked off at the hillside where I had been moments before. Moonlight played among the rocks and cacti, the cracks and the crevices. The desert at night can be soft and warm and wonderful, a playground for the gods. I had an almost overwhelming urge to slip away and fling myself across the moonlight desert floor. Eternal twilight seemed to have encapsulated the earth. For a moment, I wanted badly to be soft and weak and bathe helplessly in the soft, shimmering silver light.

Melissa's voice shattered the spell. She was speaking more slowly now, as though her body had slipped into a different rhythm. The cadence of her sentences was more measured, more sure, as if she had magically matured in the passing of a moment.

"They want you to play the game. If you don't play the game they beat you. I got tired of the game, so I didn't want to play anymore. They didn't like that, so they beat me."

The words were dry as the desert, emotionless sentences that told a story without pride or passion.

I leaned my head against the screen that separated us. "What game is that, Melissa?"

"Drugs, the party that never ends. They give you your daily dosage of the drug of choice and you make all the guests happy. It doesn't matter whether they're young or old, fat or thin, black or white, man or woman, you make them happy."

"You did that?"

She paused before answering, and I heard something scuttle in the sagebrush behind me, a wild creature or a prowling tom cat. I thought she wasn't going to respond, but before I could ask again, she answered. "At first it was fun. All that freedom, all the excitement, all shiny and new and hanging up there for me to pluck, just like a big juicy apple. Then I don't know. I got sick on some of the dope and I got tired of always being used. Every opening of my body was sore where somebody had stuck something up me. The whole concept simply got old in a hurry. Or maybe I just got old, real fast."

"Who runs this place?"

She hesitated for a moment, gathering her thoughts. "I'm not sure. I never really met him except for a minute at a party, and then I was half stoned, but I think the one they all answer to is a man named Rizzo."

"Rizzo as in a nickname, or is Rizzo short for Rizzocotti, Peter Rizzocotti?"

"I don't know." She answered in a scared little girl's voice. Something in my tone of voice had frightened her. That wasn't all bad. If we were talking about the Pete Rizzocotti I knew, we were talking big trouble.

Rizzo, as he was called by associates, hangers-on, and what passed as his friends, was a big-time mobster who had his nasty sticky fingers in a lot of pies. Nichols had told me once that Rizzo was a behind-the-scenes mover and shaker in both Reno and Vegas. I had heard through the grapevine and my contacts who dabbled in such things that he did a bit of loansharking, money-laundering, and, in his younger and more reckless days, prostitution and the odd spot of blackmail. He was rumored to have a nasty streak a yard wide, but he also was clever, had friends in high places, including lady luck. He had dodged a couple of indictments and beaten at least two good prosecutors I knew. Rizzo was bad news all the way around.

"Mr. Sanchez, are you okay?" Melissa's voice broke in on my ruminations.

"Yeah, I was just thinking about Rizzo."

"You make him sound like strychnine or arsenic. You know, a poison."

"He is, and we'd better get out of here. Come on, lift up the screen and climb on out."

Melissa looked around behind her on both sides. I didn't know what she saw, but she turned her head back toward me and said, "You go ahead. I'd better stay here." An element in her voice said I was abandoning her to a certain death.

We all are going to die somewhere, sometime. I just didn't want it to be here and now for either of us. "Come on. I'm not leaving without you."

"Go. I'd only slow you down. I'm not moving too fast these days."

"Come on, damn it. I can't leave you here. You said yourself that you were sick of it. I'm giving you the chance to get out of here and start over."

"Do I have to go to my mother's?"

"Not if you don't want to."

I heard the window screen work its way up the track. I put out my left hand to help Melissa down and never heard him coming. The back of my skull just suddenly exploded.

CHAPTER 19

There was a great bell inside my head and it swung back and forth slowly, with great solemnity. Each time the clapper hit a side of the bell I felt like my skull would explode. I lay very still and tried not to breathe so very hard. The bell rang again and all was black.

The next time I saw the light the bell wasn't as loud. I opened my eyes just a bit and let in a wedge of the light. For several seconds I thought the top of my head was going to come off, but the pressure and pain soon began to ease and I opened my eyes the rest of the way.

I had to blink a couple of times to clear the blurring. Then I wasn't sure I was glad I had. The Oriental chauffeur was seated across the room from me with a machine pistol lying across his lap. His finger was on the trigger. A second man, half hidden in the shadows, leaned against the closed door. Something metallic glistened in his hand.

Melissa was sitting in a folding metal chair a couple of feet to my right. A silver-haired man who looked vaguely familiar stood behind her. His hands were on her shoulders. She looked as if she had been crying. He had a smirky grin on his well made face. I wanted to get up and knock it off, but my legs wouldn't cooperate. I managed to sit up, but that was it. For the moment.

The man behind Melissa said something, but my hearing was all fuzzy and I picked up only distorted sounds. I tried to speak, but my tongue was thick and twisted like the gnarly roots of a Florida cypress tree. It came out something like "hungh".

All three of the men laughed at me. Melissa just looked as though she was going to be sick at her stomach. I looked down at the floor and watched it spin for a long time. I wanted to know what time it was, but my watch was missing, as was my wallet. I licked my lips and tried to swallow some of the cotton that was clogging my throat.

"Who stole my wallet?" I asked thickly.

"Nobody stole anything, Mr. Evans," the silver-haired man said smoothly. His voice was as soft and supple as well-oiled leather. "We just wanted to know who was paying us a visit. Uninvited, I might add."

"I heard your hospitality sucked and I thought I'd find out for myself. The critics were right."

He laughed at me, and the others took their cue and joined in. "There are any number of people who would disagree with you."

"Yeah, hoods like you and Rizzo."

"I'm afraid you are very much mistaken, Mr. Evans." There was iron showing through the leather now. "Some of the most prominent people of this state, in fact the entire southwest, have visited us here."

"I didn't realize this part of the country had sunk so low."

He ignored my barb. "And why did you pay us a nocturnal visit, my friend?"

"I wanted to check out the fun and games for myself, and I'm not your friend."

"Are you my enemy?" He edged a step closer to me. The Oriental took a half step to his right to make sure he had a clean line of fire. The machine pistol rose to a firing position.

"I doubt you have any real friends," I sneered.

He took another step, stopping only a foot away from me. He looked like a giant from where I was sitting. Part of me felt like a little child looking up at his dad. That was probably the way I was supposed to feel.

"What I have is no concern of yours, Evans." His voice was as hard as the rocks on the hillside I had left a little while ago.

He squatted on his heels until his face was level with mine. His eyes of blue ice looked squarely into mine. "Now what I want to know is why you are here." He gave me a smile as phony as a three dollar bill. "Believe me, it would be in your best interest to be truthful with me."

"You wouldn't know the truth if it bit you on the ass, you cocksucker."

Faster than I could blink he backhanded me across the mouth. I could taste the dark coppery blood that trickled from my lips. I waited until the little stars quit whirling in the black void before I said, "Better watch that temper. It's going to get you in trouble, as if you weren't in enough already."

"What kind of trouble are you talking about? The kind a washed up, half-crazy private eye can cause me? Don't make me laugh."

"You may be crying before the law gets through with you and your playmates."

He stood up and kicked me in the ribs, hard. I had to fight to keep from falling into the blackness. Nausea rolled over me in waves. As if I were on a distant planet, I heard him faintly say, "Take him out, Lee. And you and Miller find out all he knows, then get rid of him."

79

He rabbit punched me and things went a little crazy. I couldn't be sure if I heard the rest or imagined it. I thought I heard him say "Come on, Melissa."

Maybe she said, "Yes, Daddy."

*   *   *

The morning breeze that blew across the desert was soft and sweet and cool against my cheek. I savored it. It might be the last I would ever feel in this life.

Dawn was just breaking at the top of the hills that formed the eastern border of my life. The Oriental had his machine pistol in my back. We marched in tandem toward a low slung grove of mesquite trees and pinion pines. The sun was in my eyes and I had to squint as I picked my way among the rocky outcropping that poked its way through the sand that lay in thick layers along the dry creek bed. Out of the corner of my right eye, just at the extreme edge of my peripheral vision, I could see the shadow of Lee's partner. The man was always in shadow, or merely one himself. I half doubted that he was real. I had no such illusion about the rifle he carried. The glint of sunlight off the barrel was real enough.

A strong sense of exhilaration rippled along my network of heightened senses. Wonderful how the distinct possibility of a certain and sudden death made everything somehow so very much more real. Probably it was simply my imagination, but it seemed to me as if I could feel every separate grain of sand through the soles of my shoes.

Just inside the soft shade thrown by the trees, Lee ordered me to halt. His voice was soft and sibilant, like a woman's or a cat's. I turned and faced him. My back was against the gnarly trunk of a mesquite tree. I could feel the rough bark through my cotton shirt.

"Why did you come?"

"Because. I wanted to." I was trying to needle him, provoke him into the mistake that would give me even the slimmest chance to escape.

He didn't bite. "Who sent you?"

"The Little Shepherd of Kingdom Come."

His forehead wrinkled momentarily in confusion. Then, realizing I had been ragging him, he struck out suddenly with the muzzle of this pistol. A cloud of pain burst open behind my eyes when the metal mashed against my nose. I could feel the blood come slowly from my right nostril like a thick red worm. I licked my upper lip and tasted its sweet, warm coppery taste.

When the ringing in my ears subsided I could hear, or maybe sense, that the shadowy one was closing in on my left, just outside my field of vision. It was strangely quiet in the little grove that morning. No birds sang, no insects chirped. Though the sunlight merely dappled the ground at my feet, I was suddenly very warm. Rivulets of sweat ran under my arms and down my spine.

I wanted to get both Lee and the shadowy man with the gun in my field of vision. I began to slowly circle to my left. Lee moved with me like a tail on a kite. The other man stood as still as the fixed point of the rusted compass I had carried back in the fifth grade. The trees were more sparse here and the sun was hot now on the side of my neck. I kept moving to my left. Lee followed.

"Stop."

"Why, so you can shoot me?"

"I'm going to anyway." He grinned at me, his teeth wide and white against the sallow flesh. "But first you're going to talk."

"About what?" I was stalling, trying to buy enough time to find a miracle. Trouble was, it seemed to be a very poor season for miracles.

"I want to know why you came, who sent you. Tell me and I just might let you live." His soft voice hissed like a snake in the underbrush. He was lying through his false grin.

The second man floated into my field of vision. He was taller than I had thought, younger too. He couldn't have been much over twenty-one. The rifle cradled in his arms made him as real as death.

"A stranger sent me."

"Who? Who is that stranger?" Lee blinked furiously against the morning light like an owl disturbed at high noon.

I stopped. "Someone you don't know." I had things set up as good as I could hope for. Now all I needed was my miracle. I thought about praying, but I hadn't since 1989. It seemed pointless. If there was a God, I figured He would judge me as sucking up in an emergency. Besides, I belonged to the church of self-help.

"I said, who is that stranger, that stranger who sent you?" Lee was angry now, I could hear venom in the hiss. I could also hear a rattling in the bush off to my left. Probably a packrat or a jackrabbit. He should be getting the hell out of Dodge if he knew what was good for him.

"Answer me, man. Don't try to play stupid little word games with me." Lee's hand trembled minutely with anger. His accent became more pronounced. He came a step closer, then two. Now he was close enough for me to see his finger tighten on the trigger. I could still see the other man. In fact, he appeared to have edged a step closer himself. I desperately needed a diversion. A small twig snapped somewhere behind the narrow band of mesquite. Lee slid his left foot to within a yard of me. One more step and I would have to make some sort of move, diversion or not. It played hell with my nerves, thinking that my life might depend on the next move of a packrat.

The barrel of the machine pistol swung upwards. Now I was looking straight into the round black hole of death. All it took was the slightest squeeze on the black trigger and a bullet was going to go into my eye, through my brain, and out the back of my skull. A swift and certain death. I acknowledged that we all had to go sometime. I just wasn't sure I was quite ready for it to be here and now.

"All right, Lee. You win. It was Brown." I said it with a slow, casual drawl that I hoped sounded more convincing to the two men than it did to me.

I watched a pattern of puzzlement spread across his slightly flattened face. When it reached his eyes he said, "Who's Brown?"

The gun wavered slightly as he spoke. I had made up my mind to take my chances at the first opportunity. It wasn't there yet. Though it wavered, the gun never left my face. Just at the edge of my field of vision I could see the rifle. The blue barrel with the black hole had me hypnotized. In the absence of action, I kept talking. "Mike Brown, you know him."

Lee shook his head from side to side. Again the gun wavered, again not enough.

"Stays down at the Silver Cactus a lot. I think he might own a piece of the action."

I could almost see the wheels turning in his head. The black hole slipped a little farther south. I tensed my calf muscles. Another two inches and I would spring. I planned to go for his gun and use his body as a shield. Luck might be with me, you never knew. I once played poker with a man who drew two royal flushes in an all night game.

Lee started talking, and the gun stopped moving. "Yeah, I think I know who you're talking about. Do you, Mitch?" He asked the question out of the corner of his mouth. His head turned slightly to his right, but the gun never left my face.

"White hair, humping a redhead with big tits?"

"Sounds like him. He's got a mane of silver hair and keeps company with a redhead with a great figure. Can't say more than that." I hated to bring heat on Brown, but my brain wasn't working well in the surreal presence of its own death. The sun grew hotter as the morning grew older. Sweat ran like a river down my back. I wondered when the packrat was going to move again.

Lee blinked as sunlight slid over the top of the lines of mesquite. "What does Brown want?"

"He didn't say, just paid me to come out here to do a little surveying. Check out the lay of the land and which way the wind was blowing. That kind of thing."

"Must want a piece of the action," Mitch growled.

"Maybe," was all I said before the packrat moved again.

The rustle was louder this time. It sounded as though it came from behind a low mound of white sand and dust that supported a trio of scraggly brittlebrush and an outcropping of rock shaped roughly like an Egyptian pyramid. Lee heard the noise this time too. I saw his head jerk in the direction of the noise and the gun waver in his hand.

I exploded toward the Oriental. The two steps seemed like an eternity. I kept waiting to feel the white heat of a bullet as it tore my flesh apart. Out of the corner of my eye, I caught a brief glimpse of a dark object about the size of a bird whirling low through the air. Something in its wobbly trajectory told me it wasn't a bird, or at least not a healthy one, but I didn't have time to think about it.

My right hand closed on Lee's right wrist just as the gun went off. At so close a range it was nearly deafening and I could feel the kick of the pistol in Lee's hand. He cursed and we fell to the ground as he hit me on the forehead with his left fist.

We fell apart upon impact and the gun went flying from his hand. I wondered where Mitch was, but I didn't stop to find out. Instead I dug a left into the softness below Lee's ribs and flung a right at his chin. That missed but caught him in the throat. I heard his short gasps for air and then felt his finger dig at my eyes.

Blindness is an enraging concept. I jerked my head up and felt the top of my skull connect with the soft tissue of his nose. His elbow harpooned me in the mouth and our blood mingled in the tan sands of the desert floor. I rolled on top and grabbed his throat. He writhed like a snake beneath me. There was a feminine aspect to his movements that made me nauseous and I hit him in the face with my right fist again and again and again.

Suddenly, he was as still as petrified wood. I turned to find Mitch, the man of mystery. He was yards away, just beginning to rise up one knee and wiping ineffectively at a jagged cut above his right eye. A sharp-edged black and tan rock, about the size of a paperback book, lay at his feet. His rifle lay in the dirt.

I scrambled off the supine Lee and charged ferociously toward the kneeling man, moving as if my life depended on it. The sand was soft and loose and deep between us. It was like trying to run through warm mud. Mitch saw me coming out of his good eye. For a second, he hesitated between reaching for the rifle and setting himself to meet me. The delay was fatal.

Two steps away, I dove for him, cracking into his body just as his desperate fingers closed on the rifle. My shoulder cracked into his jaw and my fist hammered at his left ear. He screamed in pain and squeezed the trigger. The report of the rifle was deafening. I sank a left hook into his gut and heard the air whoosh out of his lungs. He banged a left off the side of my head, but there was little power in the punch. I wrenched the rifle from his feeble fingers and whipped the barrel against his jaw with all the force I could muster. He groaned and started to fall away from me. I hit him between the eyes with the rifle butt as he fell.

Melissa came up trembling out of the brush. Her lips quivered as she tried to smile. Her mouth opened as though she was going to speak, but no words came.

When I had gathered enough of my breath and wits I asked, "Are you all right?"

She nodded, and for the first time, her eyes met mine. Intelligence and fear fought for control. "I'm okay," she finally managed to squeeze out.

"I'm not complaining, mind you, but what ever possessed you to come out here?"

She shrugged her shoulders. They appeared to be very heavy. Her entire body seemed to droop as if the bulk of the life force that kept her erect had mysteriously exited her body. "I don't know. It just didn't seem right the way they were pushing you around and pounding on you, you know?" She tried to say the words with a light air but was too emotionally battered to carry it off.

She trembled again, more violently than before, then sat down suddenly on a large flat rock lightly dusted with sand. I stared intently at her. One thing I didn't need if I was going to get out with a clear conscience was Melissa going to pieces on me. I wanted to ask her how she felt, but I didn't want to make her think and worry about her fragile condition any more than she was already. Instead, I responded to her question that walked like a declaration.

"I knew what they were going to do. They might have done it too if it hadn't been for your rock. That was one hell of a throw, by the way."

She looked up at me through the hair that fell wetly down her forehead and smiled wanly, "I always was a pretty fair outfielder."

I smiled back. It had been quite a while since I had smiled, and it felt strange to feel the furrows plow deep in the leathery skin of my cheeks. "Thanks."

I paused and looked around at the two men still comatose on the ground. I didn't figure I could count on them being out for long and if they didn't show back up at the ranch soon some of their cohorts in crime would come looking.

"Melissa, I hate to say thanks and run, but I'd better be pushing off. These two may come back to life any minute and we both know they have friends." I walked over to where she sat. My legs were rubbery and strangely weak. I was in post-adrenaline rush, and at my age I didn't recover from near death experiences as quickly as I had when I was a young man.

I was tempted to jostle her hair or kiss her on the cheek, but one was too juvenile, the other too familiar, so I settled for giving her a hand to shake. However, instead of shaking it, she grabbed it with both her smooth, small hands and pulled herself erect. Her legs were trembling as much as mine.

"You'd better get on back."

"No," she said in a firmer tone.

I was puzzled. "What do you mean, no?"

"I mean no. N-O. No. What don't you understand about that?" The words were harsh in her soft throat, and she heard them. She stopped and pressed her lips together. Her eyelids fluttered like wounded butterflies as she closed them. She gave me a half bow with her head as though I were some sort of father confessor. "Sorry. I didn't mean that the way it sounds. Let me explain."

She came to me softly through the thick sand. She put her right hand on my left shoulder and shaded her eyes against the sun with her left. "You've got to understand, Mr. Sanchez, I can't go back there. I just can't. I thought that place was going to be heaven on earth." Melissa looked directly into my eyes. Hers were unblinking and guileless. "You see, I found my daddy, and he lived on this wonderful ranch where they partied all the time, and the whiskey flowed like water, and they passed out the crack like candy at Christmas."

A sorrowful look passed over her face as she paused. I kept my own counsel. She swallowed and continued, her voice softer and less rhythmic than before.

"Only it wasn't paradise, or even a very nice place at all. I guess I got some bad crack one time and it made me sick. I couldn't stand it after that. Then there was that party that never really stopped and I never got to go to bed unless it was with some fat banker from Tucson or a greasy-haired, pimple faced rock star down from Los Angeles. I mean, I never got any real rest, and I was so tired, and then they started making us perform."

"What sort of performance?" There was a nasty image rolling up in my mind and I hated to ask, but I had to know.

"Sex. Sex in front of a bunch of men. Sometimes they had their girlfriends. One time they even had their wives along." She shivered at the memory. "It was bad enough to put on a show, but it got worse when they introduced audience participation. Going to bed with one of them in your own room, in the dark, behind closed doors was one thing; to go down on them before a living room full of people was something else. I had to throw up after every show, that's how sick it made me. One old fart made me eat his fat wife's pussy. My god, she had to be sixty or more. Even her pussy hair was silver. Took me over twenty minutes to get her off. Then she came like forever. Said she hadn't had an orgasm since 1995."

"Why didn't your father stop the crap?"

Melissa laid her head on one shoulder like a tired bird and looked at me out of the corner of her eye. "You don't have a clue. My father was the one who set it up." She shuddered and then started to sob softly.

I pulled her head over to my shoulder. I could feel the dampness of her tears against my neck. I turned, and like we were Siamese twins we moved in the direction of my car. "Come on. We'd better put some distance between ourselves and that bunch of sickos." She nodded against my shoulder, and we shuffled off together beneath the white hot sun of morning.

CHAPTER 20

Melissa rode with her head on my shoulder all the way on the winding back roads to town. For a long time, she only pretended to be asleep. But then about two miles out of Santa Fe, her breathing settled into a deep rhythmic pattern. She blinked and yawned when I caught a yellow changing to red on Washington Street.

She looked around as if she wasn't sure she wanted to be there. I recognized the look from my own not so distant past. She cleared the morning out of her throat and asked, "Where are we going?"

I studied the traffic light. "Where do you want to go?"

Melissa shrugged and glanced up into my face. "Got a cigarette?"

"Don't smoke. Want a cup of coffee?"

Her only response was a semi-suppressed snort I couldn't decipher. She tossed and turned her golden head and stared out her window as though we were driving by the secret of life itself.

The light changed, and I pulled away. It was still early in the morning and traffic wasn't yet heavy. Most of the tourists were still asleep or at breakfast, and only a few silver sellers had spread their blankets on the sidewalk across the square from the old Woolworth's. I turned left onto Carson, went two blocks and took another left onto Jimenez. I jockeyed the car into a vacant parking space in front of a low modern stone building that looked functional and vaguely threatening in the morning light.

"Where are we now?" Melissa asked in a voice that teetered between boredom and nervousness.

I shut the engine off. "City Annex."

She pivoted her eyes away from the window. They found my face. "Why are we here?"

"It's time to talk to the police."

"Why should I talk to them?"

"We need to stop what's happening at the ranch."

"They won't listen. Their kind never do."

"These will. I have a very good friend on the force, Sergeant Nichols. He's a good man, about as good as they get. He won't let you down."

"But my father…" Her voice broke on the last word and she blinked back the tears.

I pulled a faded handkerchief out of my pocket and dabbed at the tears. "Melissa, your father has let you down. At least twice that I know of; once when he ran off and left you and your mother, and again at the ranch. I understand that it hurts to believe it, but it's true. The man doesn't love you. Not the way a father should love his daughter. He wouldn't stop what was happening to you at the ranch, so now we have to take steps to stop him. Maybe he's sick and needs help or maybe he is beyond help. Either way, we have to stop what's going on out there, stop it before any other young girls get hurt. Think of them if nothing else."

I put a hand on the door handle. The sunlight poured in through the glass, and I felt the beads of sweat pop out on my forehead. Melissa sat for a long time with her head bowed, her hair falling down around her face like a thick golden waterfall. Minutes mounted minutes. I heard the bells of St. Leo's toll ten. When the bells were silenced, Melissa sighed once, murmured something too low for me to hear and opened the door. I followed her dark shadow into the police station.

* * *

Tiny droplets of sweat formed at the base of her hairline and dribbled slowly down the grooves of her skull until they pooled just below her eyes with the overflowing tears. We were a half an hour into one of the most emotional, to use a kind word, police interviews that I had ever sat through. Hank Nichols looked up from his notepad and gave a policewoman named Swenson a signal with his eyes. They were cold gray mirrors that revealed nothing. He turned his gaze in my direction and jerked his head toward the door where Swenson was standing guard. She and I passed on our way in and out.

A faint breeze stirred in the narrow hallway. It was just enough to stir up the dust, stale cigarette smoke, and old memories I thought I had buried forever.

I had spent just over seven years and six months in hallways enough like this one to be cousins, in some cases brothers. Hot, dry, dusty nights thick enough to choke a man, spent with prostitutes, rapists, child molesters, murderers, suicides in training, lost children, and lost souls who hadn't known where they were for so long that they had forgotten to care.

I had soldiered through for seven years, six months, six days, fourteen hours and twenty-seven minutes. I was with Hank when he got the word about his son. We, all the brothers in blue, had struggled so hard to save him. Man hours in the thousands, overtime, sweating blood, nerves worn raw, and half crazed with worry and sleep depravation. We had honestly given our best, at least I told myself that I had, and it was for nothing. All for fucking nothing.

I had screamed and cursed and broken things with Hank. We had wept together, then laughed as one; a crazy, horrible maniacal sound, more fitting for a jackal than a man.

We had both told the police psychologist, a poor lost little man himself with tortoiseshell hornrims and a ginger-colored goatee, where to stick his couch and pseudo-sympathy. Then we told that prick of a lieutenant, Birchfield, what he could do with his regulations and squad book. Four bars and a dozen double shots of the best whiskey money could buy later, Hank had finally passed out. It took me twenty, sweaty curse-filled minutes to get him to the door and into the unmarked. The fates were with me and kept my lane mercifully clean of traffic. I needed all the help I could get that night. I was driving strictly on auto pilot.

I half dragged Hank into his house, helped Linda get him to bed, drove to the station on memories, turned in my badge, and went straight to hell. Been there ever since, thank you so fucking much. No turning back for me, no sir. Old Ward Evans knew it all. Well, not quite all. I no longer was sure whether there was a God or not. Three years after, I still wasn't sure. The only thing I had decided was, if there were, He was having one fine time laughing at the wretched antics of the miserable little creatures who were trying to run the third rock from the sun.

A heavy hand on my shoulder brought me back to the reality of the moment. "You with us?" Hank's voice was heavy and tired. I could hear weariness gurgling deep in his throat.

"Yeah, I'm right here." My own voice sounded distant and tinny in my ears. I wondered if Hank noticed.

Something must have struck him as strange. "Are you sure? You seemed a bit lost there for a moment."

"Naw, I'm okay. I've just been half lost since 1964."

His chuckle was feeble. He wasn't sure how serious I was. Not knowing how to react, he plunged ahead. I knew he would, and wasn't surprised. That was Hank's methodology, when in doubt, attack. "How much of what she's saying is true?"

"Most of it, I think. Perhaps all. I don't know of any reason that she has to lie."

"Can you verify any of her claims?"

"Some of it. Certainly the part about the rubber room and the beatings, but that doesn't do you much good as I was guilty of trespassing."

"What about the drugs and the prostitution?" A flame flickered behind his eyes. Hank was death on drugs, had been since I'd known him. Fifteen years of police work made him hate the dealer more, not love the dopehead any less.

"No proof, but I'd be willing to bet half the girls were stoned. I saw a couple of roaches and what looked like a couple of bags of Mexican Brown; nothing that would stand up in court. As for the prostitution, forget it. Unless somebody taped the deal when it was cut, there won't be any record. Besides, it was probably part of the dope deal anyway, or maybe just an old fashioned political payoff. Most of the girls probably give it away anyway. You've got to go for the drugs, Hank. You had better scout out a sympathetic judge and get a warrant, and damn fast. Once they realize what has happened they're going to close that place up tighter than Fort Knox. You won't be able to find a Marlboro let alone some Mary Jane. Then, once you leave, they'll come looking for Melissa and me." I stared straight into his eyes of smoky gray iron. "I'm a pro, and I been around the block more times than I care to admit. Melissa is just a kid though. She's too damn young, and even all she's been through, too innocent to realize that it's not a game with the boys at the ranch. So you had better get on it, partner."

He ran a heavy, hairy hand across a jaw as smooth and hard as a granite boulder. "You want in on the raid?" He arched a challenge at me with his caterpillar eyebrows.

"No, thanks, but I'm going to haul Melissa back home to her mother. That will be enough of a challenge."

"What do you mean?" Hank gave me a suspicious look. I wondered if I was the origin of his suspicion.

I shrugged the suspicion off. "For some reason the kid doesn't like her mother much better than her father. But then again, name me a teenager that does. Can't say I'm crazy about the lady myself, but she is Melissa's mother, and my client."

I turned to go back into the interrogation room. Hank's heavy hand found my arm and pulled me back. Our faces were so close I could smell the Maxwell House on his breath. "You will testify though." It was more of a statement than a question.

"Yeah. Call me when you need me."

He took his hand off my shoulder. "Thanks. I knew I could count on you. Always have." His lips cracked apart in what, for Hank, passed for a smile.

"Sure," I said. And a hell of a lot of good it did you, I thought.

*   *   *

Statements taken, typed and signed, we were out the door and on our way in less than two hours. About an hour out of town I slid into a

McDonald's with a phone on a pole imbedded in one corner of the black asphalt. I grabbed us a couple of burgers, some fries, a Coke for Melissa and a large black coffee for myself.

Melissa didn't want to talk to her mother, but I dropped a quarter in the slot anyway and called Gloria Gibson collect. She sounded somewhat surprised and perhaps just a touch disgruntled to hear from me, but she accepted the charges. I gave her the three minute Reader's Digest version of the events of the past twenty-four hours. She sounded excited and I put a still reluctant Melissa on the line.

She gave me a dirty look, but was too tired to protest further. I sipped on my coffee and listened to the short end of what sounded like a one-sided conversation. At least, I sure hoped Mrs. Gibson was talking more than her daughter. Melissa's replies consisted mainly of yeahs, rights, and okays. Two minutes after she started, Melissa took the receiver away from her ear and stiff armed it over to me. She made sure our fingers didn't touch.

I stuck the phone up to my ear and watched Melissa slowly walk to the car. She took her hamburger and Coke out of the bag and slid in the passenger side of the front seat. She moved like my grandmother, and Grandma had turned eighty-five last August.

Mrs. Gibson was talking, but I wasn't paying attention and had to ask her to repeat herself. I was getting a sinking feeling that it was going to be a long drive home.

"Really, Mr. Sanchez, what is the matter with you?" There was a hardness to her tone, a strident note in her voice.

"Sorry, I was watching Melissa."

"Why, is something wrong? Is there something you are not telling me?" I could feel a foul mixture of fear and anger wafting down the wire.

"No, she's okay. At least as okay as a girl would be after what she has been through. I suspect she's just very tired."

"You sound rather tired yourself. Are you sure you're in shape to drive?"

I wanted to respond with a smart remark to the nasty tone of rebuke in her voice. Instead, I just told her I would make it. I was too tired and it was too late in the game to argue over minor points. All I wanted now was the peaceful solitude of my purple adobe.

"See that you do, Mr. Sanchez. I have paid you good money to bring my daughter home. See that you do." I stood for a moment listening to the dial tone, then I took my cooling coffee, battered body, and dented ego over to my car and slid behind the wheel. My hamburger was cold and greasy. Melissa had drifted off to sleep and all I could get on the radio was a Mexican station or some good ole gospel music. I fired the engine, shifted into drive, and listened to the soft sounds of a Spanish guitar. Another long lonely drive on the road to nowhere.

*   *   *

Melissa slept with her body leaning against mine all the way. There was no physical attraction. Rather, she was like a young kitten or puppy who was tired of being big and brave in the cruel cold world. She was simply searching for some basic creature comforts—warmth, security, and a sense of belonging—if only for a few minutes. I certainly couldn't begrudge her that.

She woke with a jerk as I eased in along the curb. The driveway was full with Gloria's Cherokee and a bright red Pontiac Firebird, last year's model. That was okay by me. I wasn't planning to stay long anyway. I kept the motor running.

Melissa rubbed at her eyes with her fists as if reality was a bad dream she could just rub away. When that didn't happen, she pressed her face against the glass in her window and stared at the house that had been her home and was to be again.

I broke the silence. "Well, here you are, safe and sound."

"Yeah. Home sweet home, ain't it." She made the words sound like a fate worse than death.

I put a hand on her shoulder. She shrugged it off but turned to look at me. Her purple eyes were as dry as desert sand. One more shot, I told myself. "Melissa, before your mother comes out the door, tell me what's wrong between you two."

A few palomino colored strands of hair had fallen down across her forehead, and she pushed them away with a quick angry movement. She struck me as a girl on the brink of boiling over, but when she spoke, her voice was under control. "There's nothing to tell, just a simple teenager versus mother battle for control."

Her voice was full of the insight of an older woman. Perhaps she had done a great deal of thinking at the ranch, certainly more than I had imagined.

She chuckled, self-deprecatingly. "My mother always wins control games, Mr. Sanchez. She's a very strong-willed woman." She gave me a long look from the deep purple pools of her eyes. "I have always found it doesn't pay to cross Gloria Gibson. That's one reason why I left. I don't know, I guess I thought that if I got far enough away and hooked up with someone else who was strong—stronger than I was, anyway—I could get away for good."

"Get away from your mother?"

"Yeah. That is exactly who I mean." She paused, and her purple gaze turned inward. "Maybe if it hadn't been for you, I could have done it. Now, thanks to you, I have to answer to that bitch."

As if she had heard her cue, Gloria Gibson suddenly stepped out the front door and began coming hurriedly down the driveway.

Certain scientists claim that there is a unique chemical reaction between two people whenever they meet. This reaction is, theoretically, a basic, instinctive sort of thing, and it never really changes—no matter the circumstances, how many times the two people connect, or how many layers of civility mark their innermost thoughts. I had yet to have a good reaction to Gloria Gibson.

She minced her way down the concrete driveway on four inch heels. She wore tight black Capri pants that emphasized the tautness of her hips and a man's white shirt, oversized and hanging loosely over her torso. Only the middle three buttons were buttoned and the twin hard brown breasts spilled out over the top. They looked for all the world like fresh rolls from a little bakery I frequented from time to time in Santa Fe. It was located on Utah Avenue next to a coin laundry that would still let you wash a load of clothes for fifty cents.

Gloria high-heeled over to my side of the driveway as if she were uncertain of what awaited her on the passenger side of life. She leaned against the driver's side of my vehicle and stuck her golden head in through my window. Her nearly exposed breasts were virtually thrust in my face. I wasn't interested. I had never been a fan of female body builders.

"Well, Mr. Sanchez, success is ultimately yours. You have brought my little girl home to me." She made it sound like a thinly veiled threat. I began to see where Melissa was coming from.

"The name is Evans, Ward Evans, and yes I've brought Melissa home, although she doesn't seem overjoyed." That last was a bit of an understatement. Melissa had retreated to the far corner of the front seat where she was half-curled into a ball. A very sullen expression played over her soft young face.

"Ah, but there you are wrong, Mr. Sanchez, uh, Evans. Melissa is always glad to see her mother. Isn't that right, dear?"

Melissa shrugged, minutely, and apparently found something very interesting in a neighbor's yard. She did not speak. Only her eyes were alive in her face, deep purple pools full of passion, and meaning, and mystery.

"Are you sure?" I had to ask.

"Of course I'm sure. Come on and get out, Melissa, and come into the house with your mother." She put a vein filled hand through the window. There was a stone the size of a marble in a designer setting of the ring on her third finger.

Melissa didn't say a word. Seconds mounted up into minutes, until the tension was as thick as an August afternoon in a blackberry patch on a sun drenched Kentucky hillside. Mrs. Gibson waggled her finger slowly at Melissa. They looked like the legs of a spider on downers.

Finally, Melissa gave a big sigh and jerked her door open. She got out quickly and slammed the door behind her. As she reached back in to get her bag, my eyes caught hers for a moment. She had something to say, but I couldn't read her eyes well enough to comprehend the message in her mind and her lips weren't moving. Our eyes held for a brief moment, then she shrugged and was gone.

I was left with a clear impression that she was disappointed in me. I watched the two golden heads walk up the driveway side by side. Gloria tried to put her arm around her daughter's shoulder, but Melissa shrugged it off. The young girl's back was as straight and stiff as the trunk of a pine tree.

Shifting in drive, I eased the Cherokee away from the curb. I never looked back. The road opened up before me like a giant vein and the traffic flowed like blood between the two white lines.

Dropping my mind into auto-pilot I drove on instinct and impulse. The traffic ebbed and rose and ebbed until, on the far side of Santa Fe, it was a mere trickle. With every passing mile the trickle thinned until, eventually, the traffic was so sparse and sporadic that the sudden sight of another vehicle was somewhat startling.

Thoughts, unbidden, drifted into the vacuum. I thought new thoughts, strange thoughts, thoughts that I had just encountered, thoughts from years ago. They eased their way into my consciousness and I let them come. I didn't encourage or discourage. I simply opened my mind and granted entry to all who desired it.

Warm air rushed in through the open window and the Firestones below me hummed the song of the open road. My eyes threatened to surrender to a natural heaviness and the eternal flukes of pain that burned within the core of my soul dimmed.

At that moment, it seemed rather funny to me, in a sad, strange sort of way, how life meandered according to its own whims. At times it stayed within its banks carving only a deeper, straighter channel. Then, without warning it rose on an unseen tide and surged out of its predictable banks, rolling across the human landscape sweeping all before out. Later, acting on a time table not revealed to man, it retreated back to the channel. Some lived, some died, and others never really knew the difference. Then there was that select group who no longer cared, if they ever had. As I drove toward the silence of my personal desert retreat, with another day slipping away between my fingers, I had no doubt as to which clan I belonged.

CHAPTER 21

Adobe baked in the late sun of a long afternoon. It was so hot I could hear the heat hissing as it rose from the parched ground. The air trembled in the fiery furnace, and vision waves were distorted at anything beyond forty feet.

My back was flat against the adobe walls on the east side of my hacienda. I sat with my legs curled up under me enveloped in shade, not that the shade made a great deal of difference. Maybe it was only 105 instead of 120 degrees.

I hadn't been out of the house much since I returned from delivering Melissa to the bosom of her mother. I hadn't made her happy, although I couldn't honestly think of a choice that made better sense. She was too young, or maybe I was too old to care for her myself. Being out on her own hadn't worked too well either. Maybe Mommy Dearest was the best choice after all; it certainly was the safest for my reputation. Not that I was particularly worried about what others thought of me. I just wasn't in the mood to deal with the law at this crossroads in my life. Right now, I just wanted to be left the hell alone while I got a few things straightened out in my life, or at least in my mind. I was a slow thinker. I had been working at this for three months before Gloria Gibson came to my door. The way it looked to me right now it might easily be another three months. So I sat with my back against the relatively cool east wall of my adobe hacienda, sipped uneagerly on tepid lemonade, and watched another day begin to die.

It was now well after five, and shadows had begun to creep across the hillside. In the darker crevasses where boulders had been split asunder, shadows merged with twilight and foretold the purple coming of the evening. In the reddened cliffs that dominated the eastern skyline a raven tried to call to its mate. The harsh croaks it made were strong testimonies to the scarred heart that still dominated my world. Sweat ran down my forehead and spine. My white cotton shirt, unbuttoned, damp with my perspiration, clung to my back like a second softer skin.

At first I thought it was a heat-distorted delusion, a mirage of mountains. Quiet, sudden movements caught my eye. A shadowy figure moved swiftly from crag to crevice to cactus. I could see that it was on two legs, but I couldn't tell if it was man or woman. Navy shadows bled deep blue images into uneven, rock strewn ground until they met and merged with the purple twilight that crept silently up the hillside.

The figure, and that's what it was, a stick figure, was at least one hundred yards away, still not halfway down my mountain, but I could see that it was moving toward me. The speed with which the figure moved told me that he or she had traveled this trail many times before and knew the way well. Despite the heat of the adobe at my back and the sun-drenched desert that still splayed out over that side of the hacienda, I felt a chill ripple down my spine.

I had an old Colt in the top drawer of the pine dresser by my bed and a sack full of bullets behind the ancient Philco radio, but I hesitated to go and get them. I had seen young children, women, and men come down and go up the hill before. They had never yet caused me any trouble. With the passing of the onslaught of surprise, I noted the steady dwindling of my intense fear. There simply was no sense of foreboding, no instinctive response to a threat. I cupped my hands around my eyes to better focus my vision, pressed my damp shirt and back against the smooth adobe, and waited.

Before knowing, there was sensing; an instinct crawling through the intestines, caressing its sensitive nerve ends, creating a vision of the quagmire of the inner self.

Sweat beaded my forehead as if it were raining.

She was less than fifty yards from the hacienda before I was sure. She emerged from a scattered colony of small boulders patterned as if they had originally come from one monstrous slab of granite that had free fallen out of the solar system and, upon smashing into my hillside, had broken into a hundred smaller rocks like so many fragments of shrapnel.

Like liquid she flowed across the sun speckled sand and rock. Her gate was unhurried, yet she covered the fifty or so yards in a brief span of time. She came without subtlety or furtiveness. She came without arrogance or ceremony. She just came. In the end, she came just the way she walked. She carried her young body with a subtle conscious pride. She wasn't obvious about it, but I knew she knew I was there.

Ten yards away, just at that point where the smoky purple shadows merged with the light brown sandy dust, she stopped. Stopped and looked at me with a level gaze. Her mahogany eyes, flecked with gold, spoke volumes, but I knew not their language. My hand felt leaden as I waved her closer.

She came with even, deliberate steps, then stopped and squatted on her heels about two arm's lengths away. Her eyes were solemn and her wide mouth firmly closed. She wore a man's red and black flannel shirt two times too big and faded by many summers, jeans with a ragged hole in one knee, and well-worn Nikes. Her bronze skin gleamed dully in the dying sun, and the waves of her dark chestnut hair fluttered in the pert breeze that had finally arisen from its lengthy siesta to join the evening. She wore no jewelry, and the color of her face was the fixed subtle bronze shade of stained glass in a Baptist church window.

"You were gone for a long time and then you came back and then you were gone again." Her voice was low, as if she were conscious of others listening, and it came from deep in the back of her throat.

"And now I am back."

"Were you on a case?"

"How do you know so much about my life?" I was a little perturbed that one who appeared so young knew so much about me.

She shrugged and wiped away a strand of chestnut hair that had fallen across her face. "There are no secrets that can be kept from the desert."

"And you are the desert."

"I am one with the desert and the mountain and the wind. This is my people's land. They are my brothers and sisters." Her eyes were cold mahogany stones. I couldn't tell if she was serious or playing me for the fool. She was deep for her age, and full of dark mysteries. Then again, I had been by myself in my purple adobe in the great unrelenting desert for a very long time. Long enough to begin to doubt myself.

Silence fell between us like the twilight that falls between the day and the night. Minutes piled up as slowly as the sands that filled the scar in the earth that ran along the base of the red granite canyon walls. The back of my throat began to feel as dry and rough as the sand itself.

"I have some sun tea inside. Would you like a glass?"

She shook her head slowly from side to side, twice.

I pushed myself off the wall and into an upright position. She stayed squatted on her heels. I felt a bit like an ogre towering over a small child. "You want to come inside? It might be cooler."

She ignored me and sat on her heels in the gritty gravel, gently rocking back and forth to a rhythm only she could feel. There was a certain light in her eyes. Suddenly she seemed as ancient and wise as a prophet of the desert. My turn to shrug my shoulders.

It was cooler inside, but the air was stale and dry, reminding me of an old man's breath, an old man who had been confined to his bed for a long time—not unlike my Uncle George. He had been grievously wounded in Korea and spent much of his adult life in a series of progressively more pathetic Veterans' hospitals.

A day old pitcher of sun tea sat under the west window on a low Navajo table worn smooth by the passage of hands and time. The lemonade at the bottom of my glass was sour and I sat it in the dish pan and crossed the room and poured myself a plastic tumbler half full of the dark brown liquid. It looked like river water I had seen once in Florida drifting over the gnarled half-exposed roots of massive cypress trees. The tea was room temperature, but damp enough to cut through the layers of gritty dust that coated the lining of my throat.

I had always enjoyed the solitude and silence of my desert adobe, but now, with a strange young woman squatted outside my door and refusing to enter, there was a certain sullen sadness about the room. I resisted the temptation to go to the door and call to her again. It struck me as slightly amusing that I didn't even know her name. A wave of loneliness rose like bile in the back of my throat. The tea was strangely bitter on my tongue.

CHAPTER 22

Moonlight fell upon moonlight until the lunar lit landscape cast a spell upon me. An incredibly strong urge to go back down my mountain and check on Melissa began to consume me. The girl worried me. There was wonderful goodness underneath the lonely façade, and I didn't want to see it destroyed. I had surely delivered her from temptations, but the stray thought sporadically crossed my mind that I perhaps had not sheltered her from evil.

I was restless as outside forces cast their shadows across my adobe. Women of the world were wicked. I knew that. Wicked, whether they were forty or fourteen. Melissa was somewhere in between and so were my feelings. She was young and beautiful and vulnerable, yet I felt no lust, only pity and concern, emotions that had not often frequented my mind of late. She didn't feel like my sister and I didn't see myself as her father. More like a benevolent uncle. Melissa pressed on my mind throughout the night, worrying me, disturbing my hard won solitude and serenity.

So did the other one, for different reasons. Reasons I could not accurately name, only subtly suspect as though they were shadows surrounded by a sudden mist. Those great, wide-spaced, mahogany eyes flecked with gold haunted my thoughts. Sometimes I saw them in my dreams, sometimes when I was awake. Sometimes I wasn't sure whether I was dreaming or lost in the space of my own mind.

I told myself that her mouth was too wide and her lips too full. I told myself she was skin and bones. I told myself the hot desert sun and the winds that swept across the rocks would put spider veins on her cheeks before she was thirty and transform her bronze skin to leather. I told myself she was a night walker, a witch of the desert, trouble waiting to happen. I told myself that I didn't know her name, or her family, or anything else about her life on the far side of my mountain. I told myself that only yesterday she had been a child, knowing full well that she was a woman bursting forth. I told myself a fist full of lies and half-truths, and coated all of them with the salve of reality.

On the fourth night, the moonbeams became unbearable. Forced into action, I chose what I considered to be the lesser of the evil pains. I threw a couple of clean shorts, some socks and underwear, my toothbrush and razor, and what little compassion I had left for the world in my ancient Gold's Gym bag and drove off down the hill to check on Melissa. Moonlight glowed in the path like eternity's floodlights, and I bounced crazily through the sand and rocks, driving without my headlights. The night breeze blew in softly through the open windows and gently caressed my stubble-strewn cheek. It whispered in my ear names I did not know and words I would not say, but I was afraid and longed for the silence. And I would not listen.

* * *

Sunlight poured like golden liquid through the open window of Room 14 at the Pueblo de Bandas. Juan had rubbed the early morning sleep out of his eyes and found me a smile and the room an hour or so before daylight. I lay still in the softness of my bed and watched the mid-morning sun march across the floor. When it got to the foot of the bed, I forced myself up and out.

I slid on my black running shorts and my next to best pair of Nikes. I jammed my New Mexico Lobos baseball cap on my head and headed out the door. I was running on about five hours of sleep but I had good legs. Running is strange that way; like life, you never know what the day is going to bring. Legs that are coiled springs one day are solid blocks of stone on the street the next. One morning the sunshine floods the skies, the entire heavens are ablaze; the next gray concrete clouds coat the sky.

My mind must have been full of the gray concrete. Often, I do some of my best thinking on the road, but not today. My thoughts kept drifting back to the purple adobe and the little girl in too big clothes with mahogany eyes flecked with gold.

I had come here to check on Melissa, whether she wanted me to or not. I suspected that if she knew what I was up to she would be embarrassed or angry, or both. Still I had left her once before, at her own insistence, and she had not called. But in the dim recesses of my tired old brain a growing concern that she might need me again needled the soft tissue.

My Nikes slapped on a syncopated rhythm on the ancient, cracked asphalt. The white line became an uneven blur beneath my feet. Sweat rolled down my spine and dripped from my forehead into my eyes. Tears pooled in my stinging eyes and the whole world misted into a strange ethereal place where familiar images move around unknown and vastly distorted shapes.

I squeezed my eyes tightly until there were only razor thin slits open. Open just enough to let in just the light I needed to allow me to keep running.

I run to forget. I run to remember. I run to find my soul and lose my identity. I run in the sun and the moonlight. I run in the harsh reality of daylight and the quiet softness of the coming of the gentle twilight. I run to escape all my past and to postpone all my future. In the end, though, I run simply because I must.

* * *

"You are worried, Señor?"

"What? Oh no, not really, Juan. Just thinking."

"Got a lot on your mind?" He gave me a crooked grin and a shoulder shrug that said more than words.

"You could say that." I was sitting on the low adobe fence that ran below a small stand of juniper at the back of the motel. It was hot even in the shade. The weatherman on the radio had predicted 93. He hadn't missed it by much.

"A woman?"

My turn to shrug.

"Women?"

I turned my head so that I could look him head on. Our eyes met. His were muddy brown, but they were bright, warm and friendly. Back in the eighties I had had a beagle with the same color eyes. Pickett had been a fine dog.

"You a mind reader, Juan?"

He shook his brown face from left to right, then back and forth again. "No, Señor. It is just that I have often noticed that when a man is quiet and thoughtful he has a woman on his mind. If it is not a woman, it is money. Either one can be trouble in their own way."

"True, my friend, but most of us find it tough to do without either of them forever."

Juan's soft laughter mixed with the scream of a raucous jay and the distant hum of traffic. The afternoon sweltered on in the shade of the old junipers.

* * *

The moon was just crawling up the last of the high range of hills that erupted to the east of Gloria Gibson's house. It was a full moon and only a handful of white wisps of clouds had been flying against the velvet blackness of the night sky. I killed my motor and headlights, coasting in darkness down the last slope before the sharp left that took you to the house where I hoped I would find that I had wasted a fair amount of time and gasoline and made a fool of myself once again. I had this nasty little gnawing suspicion that I hadn't.

I eased over to the curb and parked nose out, ready for a quick getaway. I was tempted to leave the key in the ignition to allow a more rapid retreat. However, I didn't know the neighborhood very well. As a compromise, I put the keys in my pocket but left the door unlocked.

Streetlights were few in the neighborhood, especially on the undeveloped lots, and at least two were burnt out or vandalized into oblivion, but the moonlight streaming down filled the gaps and I moved with short, quick steps up the street. I stayed far enough off the sidewalk to be out of the yellowish pool cast by the street lamps. The ground was somewhat uneven but not so badly broken apart that walking was difficult. The sandy soil grew little vegetation and supported only enough rocks to make it worth my while to notice.

There was a vacant lot two houses down from Gloria, and I crossed the street there, running as quietly and quickly as I could. I swung wide behind the next two houses, keeping an eye out for stray toys and unidentified barbecue pits. I had a bad moment at the next to last house when a Pekinese started yapping madly. Hunkering down behind a creosote bush, I was grateful when the aggravated owner called the dog in with a profane oath.

No one at the Gibsons seemed to take any notice. The only lights showing were in the back of the house. Bedrooms was my guess, and I covered the last thirty yards on tiptoe. With my back against the still warm bricks, I realized I had been holding my breath and paused for a moment to get fresh air into my lungs and my breathing under control.

Seconds slid into minutes and no cry of alarm came, no light flickered on the porch. Forcing myself to wait until I silently counted five hundred, I tried to analyze the situation.

Stupidity ran like ice water through my veins. A careful man would have drawn up and rang the doorbell like a visiting deacon. A deacon I wasn't, never had been, wasn't going to be. According to my religion, deacons never got to the real truth, never found out about what really went on in the hearts and souls of the congregation once they got behind closed doors.

Verse nineteen of the thirty-seventh Psalm tells a great truth about more of us than we want to believe: "They shall not be ashamed in the evil time." We were in the evil time, I knew. I had seen it. Seen it through the peephole of life, looked at the darkness through the window panes of sin, stuck a bloodshot eye against the keyholes of the backdoor of depravation.

No, I wasn't strictly an honorable fellow, rather a searcher of the truth and dispenser of justice tempered with mercy. Who better to know the sins of the sinners but the chief sinner himself?

CHAPTER 23

As silently as I could, I worked my way down one side of the Gibson house. Remnants of the heat of the day still lingered in its bricks. They were as warm as human flesh beneath my palms. I moved from the back to the front, taking care to avoid the scattered patches of white gravel and stray yucca and cactus that comprised the landscaping. For a home in this neighborhood, the plantings were meager.

The lighting wasn't any better. The nearest street light was across the pavement and thirty yards to the south. Neither Mrs. Gibson nor her neighbor had invested in the sensory lighting that was suddenly stylish with the moderns. My eyes gradually became accustomed to the near darkness and I made my way without particular difficulty.

The only bad moment I had came as I approached the left front corner of the house. A car suddenly swung onto the street from an adjacent one, its headlights penetrating the blackness like twin airport searchlights. I crouched in the jagged shadows of a four foot high saguaro and tried to make myself small and dark, just simply another segment of the nocturnal landscape. The car moved on without pausing and I quickly crossed the front lawn, staying close to the bricks and thin welcoming shadows.

Neither side of the house was productive. All the shades were drawn and the windows firmly shut. Few lights were on inside the house, and their meager patches of light offered no clues. I could discern no noises emanating from inside, save for the faint murmur of a television set tuned in to a sitcom. The muffled canned laughter sounded phony in the clear desert air.

I saved the back side of the house for last. I hadn't been there enough to know my way around, and I had an unpleasant vision of taking a wrong step and doing a belly-buster in the pool. However, my lack of success up to that point impelled me to either try it or take my act back home.

The latch on the wooden door that opened onto the pool and patio needed oiling and squeaked slightly as I slowly swung it open. Deciding discretion was the better part of valor, I opted for the rather inglorious method of crossing the patio on my hands and knees feeling carefully for the smooth sides of the pool before I moved forward. This method of traveling dictated slow going. The rough pebbly textures of the patio poked at my palms and knees as if to remind me of the extreme foolishness of any evasive action should the patio lights suddenly came on. That was a long shot, though. I had been in foolish, foolhardy positions before.

No lights flashed on, no one cried out, and I kept myself out of the pool. So far so good, but I wasn't making any real progress. My back was to the wall, literally; I could feel the warmth of the bricks through my shirt. I had come a long way, now I wasn't sure where I was going next. My choices were left or right. I flipped a mental coin and slid to my left.

Three steps later I was under what I guessed to be a bedroom window. The overhead bulb was dark, but light drifted in from beyond the room. Accompanying the lights were occasional sounds. The intermittent sounds were just faint enough to be undecipherable, just loud enough to be interesting. Interesting enough to drive me reckless.

Security systems were the rage in affluent Southern California, more of them were being installed on a daily basis in Santa Fe and Albuquerque. Still, probably less than ten percent of New Mexico's population had them. That percentage might rise to twenty or twenty-five in an affluent neighborhood like this one, but I figured the odds were still with me. Besides, I would have tripped a good system fifteen minutes ago, and there were no police sirens wailing in the distance. I eased out of my crouch and got a good grip on the window ledge, pulling myself up until I could see into the room.

It was a smallish room furnished with a single bed, a black wooden dresser, and a huge Boston fern on an antique black lacquered stand. There was an old Philco radio, unplugged, on the dresser and a thirteen inch Mitsubishi TV. There was a cupboard in one dark corner and a basket of folded clothes in another. The cover on the bed was smooth and throw pillows bunched together against the headboard. I figured it for a spare bedroom. I dropped back to the ground and went to look for a ladder, or at least a chair to stand on.

I recalled seeing the outline of some moderately large object near the pool. This turned out to be a beach chair, too flimsy to hold my weight. There was a metal table too big to carry and too noisy to drag across the poolside patio. I was beginning to despair when I brushed up against a good-sized metal trash can. I lugged it over to the bedroom window without falling down or losing the lid. Setting the can on the gravel, I worked it back and forth until it was firmly anchored. Then, I clamored on top.

There was a large mirror on the back of the dresser. A hard looking man with a droopy mustache and a haggard look stared back silently at me from the depths of the glass. I gave him my best lopsided grin and pushed on the window. My luck was in—it was unlocked. Out of the corner of my eye, I caught the foolish man now grinning back at me from the mirror.

Light fell in strange modernistic patterns across the plush charcoal gray carpet. I followed a shadowy path across the room. At the doorway, I paused and listened intently. I could hear more than I could see, at least for the moment. My field of vision was limited to this one small room and about five feet of the hall on either side of the door. Sounds, distorted by distance and plasterboard though they were, traveled significantly farther.

Except for the quiet hum of a giant air conditioning unit, the sounds were intermittent and strange. I could hear, at irregular intervals, popping or smacking sounds. Low muffled moans, and once, a high pitched squeal of female laughter. It sounded like Gloria Gibson to me, but then again, my imagination could have been messing with my mind. It often does.

No shadows shaped like a man, or a woman, crept down the hall. No door screeched open, and I ventured a quick glance down both directions of an empty hall. No voices challenged my right to be there, and I stepped out of the darkness and into the light.

The noises I could not identify seemed to be coming from my left. The hall was carpeted in a good quality indoor/outdoor type carpet with enough padding underneath to silence my footsteps. It appeared as though the hall was in the shape of a big U with squared off ends and I was at the base of the U. A half dozen or so steps later, I took the right turn and headed up the left side of the hall, which looked to run the length of the left side of the house.

Almost immediately, there was a door on my right. I wasn't ready for a room so soon, and it gave me a terrific start. However, it turned out to be a bathroom full of shampoo, soap, towels, toilet paper, and not much else. Ten feet further and across the hall was another room. The volume of the sounds was increasing, but a quick glance told me they weren't coming from this room. Instead, it looked like a girl's bedroom. Bare-chested young men sporting long hair and guitars cradled in their arms like machine guns stared down at me from their places of honor on the wall. A sundress was carelessly slung over a chair, and lipstick tubes, powder puffs, perfume bottles, and assorted pieces of jewelry fought for supremacy atop the dresser. One tennis shoe stood silent sentinel just inside the door. My guess was Melissa's room, but I didn't have the time to check it out. I kept moving down the hall. The sounds were coming faster, louder, more clearly. The hairs on my arms and at the base of my skull stood at attention.

The Tremolos had a hit back in the 1960s titled "Silence is Golden". Well, it sure was for me. I was grateful for the soft carpet, as the noises were emanating from the room just ahead on my right. I crept forward on tiptoe like a burglar trying to slip out of the master bedroom, with the master already restless in the bed.

The door to the room of noises was ajar about ten or twelve inches. I couldn't see much through the aperture. Light spilled from around the edges of a ninety degree turn created by a wall of dark wood paneling. I thought thin, sucked in my stomach, and squeezed through the opening as quietly as I could. It was a tight fit, my chest brushing against the door, but the heavy door didn't move. If it noticed I came at all it didn't make a sound. I had the feeling that it had seen stranger sights than me passing by.

Noise accompanied light in the equation and both originated from beyond the other side of the dark wall. The paneling was superb walnut, and the carpet was three inches thick and looked brand new. I moved as quickly and silently as a November cloud. I went low and tight up against the wall to keep my shadow to a minimum. I had a .38 special in my pocket and a fistful of fear in my heart.

Pausing at the corner, I eased my head slowly around the corner. An old memory of a kid's game and seeing if the coast was clear came floating unbidden across my mind.

The coast was clear. The other occupants of the room were far too occupied with their own games to pay any attention to me. For that, I was grateful. I had lived more years than I cared to count and had covered my share of rough territory and seen some strange sights, but I wasn't prepared for the room ahead.

A man was tied tightly to an upright wooden chair set on a low wooden platform. Most of his back was angled toward me and I could easily see the welts and bruises that crisscrossed his back in a weird herringbone pattern. Blood oozed from a half dozen welts. His arms and legs were purple above and below the manila ropes that bit tightly into his arms and legs. His fingers were thick and dark like blood sausage. His bald head was bowed over a sunken chest and a flabby belly. The eye I could see, his right, gazed with rapture at his groin.

It was easy to see why. Melissa, clad only in a chain choker as thick as my belt and six inch stiletto heels held his erect penis in her soft, warm mouth. She moved her head rhythmically up and down. Every few seconds her little pink tongue slipped out and licked the engorged member like it was an all day sucker. He groaned softly every time the tip of her tongue caressed the head of his penis.

Behind Melissa was the real surprise. Melissa herself was draped over an old leather pommel horse with sawed off legs. Her young breasts, pulled by gravity, hung from her chest like ripened fruit. Her plump bottom stuck straight up in the air.

Gloria Gibson was behind her daughter. She wore big gold bracelets like wristbands on her arms and huge golden hoops within hoops within hoops of earrings, dangling six inches below her earlobes. Except for the thigh high shiny red latex boots, that was all.

All, that is, but for the foot long black strap-on dildo that looked as thick as my wrist. Her big, breasts quivered with each thrust of the massive dildo into Melissa's anus. Her hands roamed her daughter's back as though she were reading Braille. A nasty, black leather whip hung loosely from the strap on her left wrist like some obscene python. Gloria's eyes were closed in ecstasy, her mouth parted as she greedily sucked in air. Melissa's eyes were glazed over in a parody of self-degradation. Her body shuddered with each thrust her mother made.

My head spun like a world whirling through space on a broken axis. The contents of my stomach surged upwards and scoured the back of my throat raw. My breath came in shallow, uneven gasps. The glaze that covered Melissa's eyes seemed to have spread to my mind. Trying to gather my thoughts, I forced my eyes back to the center of the room.

Timing, after all, is everything. Mine was everything bad. I was just in time to catch Gloria Gibson in the throes of an orgasm. She whined shrilly in ecstasy. I was suddenly so very tired of the sickness. My only choice was to do something about it personally, now, or retreat, perhaps forever, to my purple adobe in the silent desert.

While I stood there with my brain benumbed into neutral, the man's body jerked as he came. He groaned very softly to himself. Melissa's slender throat contracted as she swallowed the fat man's cum.

Rage turned the image crimson, and I rushed across the room like a maddened bull. I was mad, goaded beyond normal boundaries of the rational side of life.

Only in the final stride were they alert to my presence. The fat man saw the fist that crashed into his right eye only milliseconds before the impact. I followed the right with a left that smashed into the side of his exposed jawbone and sent him reeling. His flaccid penis dangled like wasted flesh between his flabby thighs. He staggered blindly across the room and crashed full steam into the concrete block wall. His head thumped like an overripe melon against the paneling and he slumped to the floor, not knowing or caring where he was.

The flesh that stretched across my cheekbone ripped apart under the force of the leather whip. I roared in pain as tears filled my eyes. I raised my right arm to ward off the next blow.

"I'll show you, you interfering son of a bitch." The whip fell like liquid fire and brushed my arm. She cackled with delight.

To stand still was to issue an engraved invitation to disaster. I lunged forward and tripped over Melissa's outstretched legs. My head smashed onto the floor and stars filled my eyes. The whip lashed against my left ear and there was only a pool of dark blood and silence.

Half-deaf and nearly blind, I stretched out my right hand and felt the leathery smoothness of Gloria Gibson's leg. The whip smashed across my shoulders like a thunderclap from hell, but I hung on grimly and jerked with everything I had.

She sat down with a resounding thud and a heartfelt, "Goddamn." Her eyes were suddenly full of surprise and shot with fear.

I scrambled forward and drove a shoulder hard into her full chest.

She went backwards like a toppled totem pole and screamed, "Don't, please," but I hit her anyway, a glancing blow off the side of her head. I had never hit a woman before, but she was a pureblood bitch. I felt only the anger. I no longer cared.

Her fingers clawed at my eyes like talons, and I felt my hot blood stream across my cheek. She was cussing and swearing, and begging me seductively to stop all in the same breath. I tried to shut her up, but she jerked her head and I smashed her nose instead. She banged the butt of the whip against my temple, and I smashed home a right solidly between her eyes. I followed this with a left that loosened her teeth and slit her upper lip and the fight left her. She pulled her legs up and together in the fetal position and sobbed softly for mercy. I looked at Melissa, still hung out to dry over the vaulting horse. The big black dildo was still strapped between Gloria's legs. I found no mercy in my soul.

What I found, in the top drawer of a two-drawer filing cabinet, were two pair of handcuffs, a slim packet of one hundred dollar bills wrapped in a rubber band, a half dozen pornographic films, a studded dog collar, a blonde wig, a ball gag, and, finally, a ledger two-thirds full of names, dates, amounts, and services rendered. The key to several futures nestled innocently in the book. The entries went back for months on end and listed in graphic detail the personal peculiarities of a significant number of individuals. Gloria had been very sure of herself; names were written without code or subterfuge of any kind. A few were prominent enough that even I recognized them. They had no way of knowing, but dark clouds were massing on the horizon of their futures. I left the ledger open on top of the file cabinet.

Into one pair of handcuffs, I joined fat and flaccid and Gloria in unholy union. The other pair I used to chain Gloria to one of four large steel beams that were strategically placed in the wall. He was still kissing the wall and knew not what I was doing. She looked up at me with venom in her eyes that belied the seductiveness of her words.

"Let me loose, Evans, and I'll forget the whole thing," she lisped through rapidly puffing lips.

"I wouldn't forget."

"I can help you forget." Her firm breasts were pointed upwards and thrust toward me as a sort of fleshy peace offering.

"You can't help me do a damn thing. Besides, I wouldn't trust you as far as I could throw him."

Her quick mind was still functioning. "I can pay you."

"No."

"Pay you very well," she purred.

"I wouldn't take your filthy money."

"You already have," she sneered.

I choked back hateful words and an almost overwhelming urge to slap the sick smirk off her face. Instead, I forced the ball gag in her mouth and pulled the clamps tight behind her head. Then I took her whip and rammed the rigid handle as far up her anus as it would go. Her blue eyes screamed at me in pain.

Melissa was too far gone to help herself. I had no idea what she was on, or what might counteract its effects. I rummaged around in what I surmised to be her room and found some clothes that looked like they would fit. It was like dressing a life-sized doll. She moaned softly, gently to herself once or twice, but never opened her eyes.

I carried her gently to my car just before dawn. She was soft and warm and as innocent as the Sunday morning sunshine. It was almost impossible for me to comprehend that she was the daughter of the woman I had left chained to a fat bald man. A women with a dildo strapped to her womanhood, a leather whip handle up her ass, and more problems than she could imagine.

Night begets morning, and I rolled smoothly over the asphalt into the new day. On the way out of town, I made two calls. One was to Hank Nichols, the other was to Father McMichaels, my old police chaplain in Las Vegas. Hank was having his second cup of coffee. Father McMichaels had passed away last September.

CHAPTER 24

The jay sat motionless on the second lowest branch of the gnarled old oak. The tree had stood for many seasons in the wind and the sun, and its branches were twisted and twirled like broken pretzels. Here and there were gaps in the foliage, like missing teeth in an old man's mouth. The trunk was scarred by a lightning strike about ten feet from the base. An old wildfire burn blackened the base three or four feet up the trunk, but the leaves were many and green.

A car motored slowly up the long, winding asphalt path. It grated against the back of my mind like a stone being dragged across a long shard of glass. The jay didn't like it either and he had the courage of his convictions so he flapped his wings and took himself off out toward the western horizon. I sat in my cracked green leather chair by Melissa's bed and watched the long white Cadillac, sporting smoked glass clean enough to eat off, roll down the black asphalt.

Restlessly tossing in a sea of dreams, Melissa turned over so that she faced me. One slim white arm flung out in my direction. I reached down and wrapped my right hand around her fingers. Her skin was soft and silky, and the lifelines traced only faint shallow furrows across her palm.

One purple eye opened as slowly as the coming of Christmas morning. Recognition swam hesitantly through the drug induced depths to the surface. It was the first time in three very long days.

The faintest of smiles flickered across her lips and then stored away like ripples on a pond. Her voice was a whisper at the wrong end of a dead end street. "Mr. Evans, is that you?"

"It's me, Melissa. Good to have you with me. How are you doing?"

She licked her lips as if they were thick slices of wood chips, while she considered the question. "I'm not sure. I can't seem to remember how I've been lately." She shrugged. The look on her face said her shoulders weighed tons. "Is that okay?"

I felt the smile come unbidden to my lips. "Yes. I think that's all right. We'll let Dr. Christiansen tell us."

110

Melissa reluctantly raised her head and looked slowly around the small room, with its hospital bed, oak dresser, washstand, and matching leather chairs of ancient lineage. "Where am I?"

I hesitated, then decided to tell the truth. "In a room at St. Mary's of Edgewood."

The purple pupils widened. "Why am I here?"

I gently stroked the back of her hand. "Maybe we'd better wait until the doctor gets here."

As if on cue, the door swung open and two men walked in as if they owned the place. One of them did. I had seen his picture in the *Times* last year.

Dr. Christiansen was tall and lean with a sparse economy to his stride and gestures. He looked to be in his early forties. His black hair was the kind of long you get when you get too busy to schedule your next visit to the barber. It was flecked with silver, and there was a certain sag of the shoulders as if they had borne a great weight for a great time without rest. He crossed the room in a direct line, and the slender hand he extended packed a firm grip. A narrow gold band bit deep into the sparse flesh of the third finger of his left hand. His black eyes were bright and shiny as a bird's.

"You must be Mr. Evans, Ms. Gibson's benefactor." The voice sprang deep from his narrow chest and rumbled out like it came from a wine cask. The doctor should have been a senator.

"That's right, Dr. Christiansen. I'm Ward Evans."

"You know my name?" He seemed surprised but flattered.

"I read about your clinic's wonderful success percentage last fall."

He nodded his narrow head. His skull, in half-profile, reminded me of a picture of a Spartan's sculpture that had graced my high school World Civ textbook. "You must have seen the *Times*. As you may know, Mr. Evans, writers tend to hyperbole."

"There is usually a nucleus of truth."

The doctor gave me a half-smile as if I had won an unimportant point. "Granted. We have not been without our successes here at St. Mary's, but from my point of view, and it is ultimately the only one that counts around here, the only percentage of success that is wonderful is one hundred." He again gave me his quick shrug, and turned to introduce the other man. "Mr. Evans, this is—"

"Sergeant Nichols. And we know each other, Doctor. As a matter of fact, we go back a long way. Hank, how are you doing?" I gave him my right hand and got back a sack of battered bones.

"Okay. Yourself?"

"Good for now."

Hank gave me a funny look that came up from under his thick eyebrows. I ignored him. I was trying to watch Dr. Christiansen, who was pulling the other chair up close to Melissa's bedside.

The doctor took one of Melissa's soft small hands between both of his long, thin, bony ones and rubbed them gently and slowly back and forth, over and under her flesh as if he were trying to bring warmth back into a long frozen mummy. Melissa's eyelids fluttered faintly as though she were suddenly fatigued.

"And how are we today?" His voice was mellow, like fine old whiskey aging in his narrow chest.

She gave him a quick little anxious-to-please smile. "Okay, I guess," she said faintly from deep in her pillows. "Better than yesterday, anyway," she added hurriedly, her eyes darting quickly around the room to include us all in her survey.

Christiansen's eyes followed hers. His eyebrows arched in recognition as if he had forgotten Nichols and I were in the room. "Melissa, you know who these men are?"

A faint, "Yes."

"Is it all right with you if they stay?"

"Yes," somewhat more firmly.

The doctor gave us both a meaningful look. Unfortunately, I couldn't tell what message he was trying to pass. He turned his Spartan's skull back to face his patient. "What have you been doing all day, Melissa?"

She sighed softly to herself as if she had been given an exacting exam question. "Just lying here mostly, and thinking. I tried to read a little bit, but the words hurt my head and there was nothing on TV, and then Mr. Evans came so we sat for a long time together."

Christiansen smiled and patted her hand. "Did you and Mr. Evans talk much?"

Her lips paused as she considered this inquiry. "No, not really. Mostly we just sat together." She smiled up at the doctor as if she were asking forgiveness.

He smiled back and let the silence settle about her shoulders like a soft cloud, but only for a moment. Then suddenly, he shrugged his shoulders as if the weight had shifted and suddenly become too heavy for him. "Melissa, you mentioned earlier that you had done some thinking today. What in particular did you think about?"

"Oh, I don't know. Just stuff. You know, like what I was going to have for lunch and why did I have to take the pills and how long was I going to be here and when could I leave."

"And did you eat your lunch?"

"Some of it. The soup anyway. It was cream of chicken. I like that, it's one of my favorites."

"You mentioned leaving, Melissa. Do you want to leave?" The question floated as gently in the air as a feather settling on the surface of lake.

"Maybe. Someday." She paused and turned to look out the window. I couldn't see the jay anywhere. "I just don't really know right now."

Christiansen looked at the window too. His gaze had a far away aspect as if he were seeing something a hundred miles away. After a longish moment, he said, "That's okay, you don't have to be sure about anything right now. Have the dreams been back?"

From my field of vision I could see Melissa's face reflected in the clear glass of the window. I watched her eyes spread wide open and then shut tightly. In a few seconds I could hear the faint sobbing start. Christiansen quit staring through the window at a far away something that only he could see. After a bit, Nichols caught my eye and jerked his head toward the door. I followed his long dark shadow out of the room.

"That doc's a strange one." Hank Nichols' big left hand was scraping across the stubble that was already starting on his still firm jaw. Except for the crow's feet that grew around his eyes and the inch of extra flesh around his middle, Hank was holding off the scourge of the years rather well.

"He's pretty intense."

"Intense," Hank nodded his cannonball of a head in agreement. "That's the word. Intense and young. Way too damn young."

"They all look young these days, Hank. Maybe it's us who are getting old."

Hank turned his head so that he could glare directly into my eyes. "Don't start with that age shit, compadre. All I hear these days is 'Hank, you are too old to do that'; 'Hank, you shouldn't do that', 'Hank, those clothes are not becoming on a man of your age'. Well, old Hank is sick of the old crap. I say a man is only as old as he feels."

I looked up at the sky. A single white cloud, shaped a little like Oklahoma, floated on a sea of chicory blue. I laughed a little to myself. "I agree with you. Only thing is, some days I feel eighty."

"What are you laughing about?" Hank asked sarcastically. "Just 'cause a man feels rough some days is no need to laugh at him. Or call him old."

"Sorry. I wasn't laughing at you. It just struck me as funny."

"Well, it's not."

"Okay, okay." I knew from long, bitter experience not to verbally joust with Hank. He could get on a jag and stay there for days. I twisted my head so that I could see Hank's face. "By the way, I wanted to thank you for all your help with Melissa."

"No need to thank me. I was just doing my job."

"I know, but you got a hell of lot done in a hurry." I watched a hawk soar in long blue loops on the eastern sky. He rode the current of air as if it were a magic carpet. "Besides, I know you had to pull some strings. Christiansen didn't come into the picture by accident."

Hank studied the thick trunk of the oak as though it were an Etruscan carving replete with hidden meaning. Seconds ticked by like sand sifting through the hourglass. His voice was husky when he finally spoke. "What happened to that girl shouldn't have happened to anybody, especially a kid. She deserved a break. I had an opportunity."

He shrugged his shoulders and sat on the top of a wooden table that stood between two wooden benches rapidly disintegrating to splinters. I joined him. He was right. I had nothing else to say. Hank and I sat in silence as the hawk soared slowly above us in ever tightening circles. The world soared through space I couldn't fathom. The clinic baked contentedly under the morning sun.

*   *   *

I watched the sun and not my watch. It crawled its golden way with excruciating slowness across a huge blue field. There was heat to go with the light. I felt its first bead of sweat form at the base of my hairline. I waited. The sweat slowly slid south down my forehead and ran along the left side of my nose. The heat was rising on our little hillside, and my shirt was plastered onto my back.

Hank stared restlessly to my right. He was a busy man with a job that came with a built in timetable. I was an out of work private investigator lost in space with a life sentence yet to serve. I closed my eyes and tried to remember the last time I had worked according to someone else's schedule.

"Evans?"

"Yeah?"

"You asleep?"

"No. Just thinking."

He stared at an object only he could see for a few seconds, and then I heard him stand up. I decided to close my eyes and stay where I was and let the sun bake my brain for a few minutes longer. A shadow fell across me. Something rather large was between me and my sun. I slowly opened my eyes. It was Hank. I was not surprised.

He took off his hat and wiped his brow with the back of his hairy hand. "Man, it's starting to get hot out here and I need to get on back to town. Wondered if you could hang around and talk to Christiansen for me. Find out when I could have another interview with Melissa."

He squatted on his heels and brought his face to within six inches of mine. Old Spice and coffee breath blended aromatically in my nostrils.

"Ward, that girl knows a lot, a hell of lot more than she's telling me. Now Christiansen is all right. I respect his medical ethics and I understand the girl needs some time to rest and recover. Hell, you know I have her best interests at heart. A while ago you were talking about the extra effort I had done for her. But the problem is, he keeps putting me off. Talk to him for me, will you? He likes you, I can tell. Besides, you're the one that saved Melissa from that whore from hell who calls herself a mother. I know a lot already, but in order to put that bitch away for a long time, I need more."

I had a pretty good feel for what the chances of influencing Christiansen would be. No need to disappoint Hank so early in the day, though. "I'll talk to him. No guarantees on what he'll say. My experiences with doctors is that they tend to do a lot of independent thinking, and Christiansen might be a hair more independent than most."

A beefy hand clamped down on my left shoulder like a vice. "You'll do good, Ward. I've got a lot of confidence in you."

I shrugged my shoulders in an effort to deflect and depreciate his overly positive words. "We'll see what happens. No promises."

"Hey Hank."

"Yeah."

"Speaking of putting people away for a long time, what ever happened to Rizzo and that bunch out at the ranch?"

Hank rubbed a hand across his face. It looked like a sirloin steak traversing a smoked ham. "Rizzo is in parts unknown. Most of the rest made bail."

"Melissa's dad?"

"Out and about. Better watch your ass, buddy."

He gave me a wide grin that revealed a full set of large, straight white teeth and then groaned softly to himself as he stood up. "Getting old, partner. Thanks a bunch for your help." He waved a hairy paw back and forth. "Really do have to get back to town. Catch you on the flip."

"See you down the road," I said to his back that looked as big as a barn door. He walked toward the parking lot, moving as though his feet hurt him.

CHAPTER 25

"She's a long way from what you might call healthy, Mr. Evans."

"What about you, doctor? Would you classify her as healthy?"

I settled back in the soft crushed leather of the huge old dinosaur of a couch that occupied considerably more than half of one of the lime green plaster walls that barricaded Christiansen against the outside world. There was a large water stain on one wall and the plaster had started to peel. Like his patients, Christiansen's wall needed some tender loving care.

"Health is one of those words that Webster's defines, not doctors." His long slender fingers traced patterns that I couldn't see on a walnut desk. "They say that beauty is in the eye of the beholder. Sometimes I'm tempted to substitute health for beauty. I have spent most of my adult life engaged in the study of the human mind, and perhaps the only thing I can say with absolute certainty is that none of us possesses a totally healthy mind."

"But we aren't all in clinics like yours."

"No, but maybe we should be from time to time."

"Self-analysis, doctor?"

He smiled a lip thin smile of self-deprecation and nodded his head. "Physician heal thyself." He snorted and straightened in his high backed leather chair. "You must excuse me, Mr. Evans. I am a bit tired and I tend to ramble and wax verbose in that condition."

"When I was growing up, my dad used to say I had diarrhea of the mouth."

He chuckled softly. "Yeah, something like that." He rolled his big bony head back on his chair and closed his eyes.

We passed a pleasant moment of quiet companionship. The other world seemed far away, and the door was real wood and only muted slivers of sound joined us in the room. As though from a great distance I could hear the faint voice of a woman who sounded strangely like my grandmother, the one who had baked me rhubarb cobbler, not the one who had regularly striped my legs with a peach tree limb.

I broke the silence. "Sergeant Nichols would like a few minutes with Melissa as soon as she's up to it."

"I know."

"Her testimony may be essential to his case."

Dr. Christiansen opened his eyes and gave me an unhappy look. "Her emotional state is certainly essential to her future." I didn't say a word, and in a few seconds he looked out the window. He looked in that direction for a very long time, as if he hoped to find the answer to his problem or at least give me ample opportunity to leave. Neither happened, and eventually he pivoted back around and remade eye contact. The good doctor was not happy. He liked to save people, but in his own way and according to his own sense of time and order. I was threatening his world, a nasty little monkey wrench in the spokes.

"I am sorry, Mr. Evans. You and your policeman friend have been of great value to Melissa. However, you two cannot push the healing process as much as you would like to. I simply cannot allow your desire to send some soul to prison to negate all the progress that Melissa has made. A setback now could be disastrous."

"To let Gloria Gibson off would be criminal."

"You must forgive me, but I am not terribly concerned with convicting anyone. Mankind, womankind tend to bring on their own sentencing." He sighed softly, more to himself than me, and massaged his temples with the balls of his thumbs.

"Aren't you concerned with justice, Doctor?"

"A little healing garnished with mercy will more than suffice." He inclined his long, sensitive skull toward the thick door of his domain. "Now if you will excuse me, I have work to do."

I swallowed hot heavy feelings. They tasted like bile. My legs had turned to stone as I sat on the good doctor's leather chair and discussed philosophy. The lime green walls looked at me through their cracks and crevices. They looked as though they were closing in on me. When I could hear them laughing at me I pushed myself erect and walked across the floor stained by the passage of the years. Every stain seemed to contain a message. I was blinded by the light of reality and could not decipher any of them. At the door I paused and looked back. The good doctor was as still and silent as an Inca carving. My tongue trembled with the words I wanted to say. However, I was afraid. I turned and went down a long, dark hall that seemed to run for a half mile. I pushed open an oak door stained as dark as the blood of an ox and stepped into another hall bordered by the rooms of patients. On my way out I signed the visitor's book as Hubert H. Humphrey and blew Melissa a kiss through her locked door. A quickening breeze was dancing in the parking lot. It felt hot and dry on my face. The sunlight was so bright it hurt my eyes.

CHAPTER 26

On the way home I detoured by the police station. A plump lady sergeant, with bigger muscles and a darker mustache than mine, said Hank had gone to testify at traffic court. She told me how to find the courthouse and told me I could wait there or stay where I was until he returned. He was due back in an hour. I thanked her for the information and said that I would catch him later.

It was just three blocks to the courthouse and I decided to walk. The sun was hot, but a breeze was blowing down from the mountains and a few trees had sprung up along the way, and here and there a multi-story office building blocked out the light. My legs felt good, the ground was flat, and I moved along like a smoothly functioning robot, my gears lubricated by the fine sheen of sweat that formed on my skin.

Across the street from the courthouse there was a small drugstore on the corner. The bricks that encased it were old, their color faded by countless hours of exposure to a broiling sun. I empathized with them. I felt a bit faded myself after my encounter with the good doctor. I jogged across the street against the traffic flow, zigzagged through the cars and vans and trucks that slid over the asphalt like salmon going back to their birthplace to spawn.

Just inside the door it was dark and smelled of dust and medicine and dreams dying hard. The floor consisted of oil coated boards. They looked damp and dark, and they creaked beneath my feet. There was a long black and white Formica counter on the left side of the narrow store. Eight stools, covered in cracked red leatherette, stood at attention in front of the counter. They were all empty. A tall, lean man with unhinged ears and faded red hair stood behind the counter. He eyed me cautiously over the top of his *National Geographic*. As I crossed the room I could see it was the May, 1997 issue.

"Good morning." His voice creaked like his floorboards.

"Morning."

"What'll it be?"

"Cup of coffee."

"For here?" His tired eyes swept lightly across the parade of stools.

I shook my head. "Make it to go."

"Business good?" I asked his back. He was thin, almost microchip flat and his pants sagged in the rear like a teenage boy's.

"Not like it was before," he said over his shoulder.

"Before what?"

He turned and put a Styrofoam cup of coffee on the counter between us. The liquid was black as oil and bubbles foamed on top like Kentucky horse piss. Contrails of steam rose like smoke signals. I couldn't decipher the code.

"Before Wal-Mart." He made the name sound like an obscenity.

"Hurting your business."

"Mine and everyone else's." he ran a vein-filled hand along a leathery cheek. "My grandfather opened this store in fifty-four. I've been here since seventy-six. Won't last out the year, barring a miracle. And those are few and far between, at least in my life."

"That bad."

"Worse." There was a certain sourness in his voice and on his face. "They opened a year ago in March on the west end of town. I've lost money every month since, and I wasn't making much to begin with."

"You can't compete with some special service, free delivery, something like that?"

"No more than I can stop an avalanche. Wal-Mart's just too goddamn big and too goddamn greedy." The light in his eyes turned inward and his head swung back and forth, very slowly as if it were an old mission bell and he was afraid that too vigorous movement would crack it.

He smiled, just a little, and more to himself than me. "Tell the truth, guess I'm just too darn old and discouraged to care much anymore." He looked up at me. His eyes were hard and flat as twin chunks of ancient iron. "That'll be one dollar for the coffee. I threw in the bitchin' for free."

I dug a dollar out of my billfold, laid it on the polished counter and picked up my coffee. Then I walked back over the protesting floorboards and across the street. This time I waited for the light.

Someone had put a wooden bench in the corner of the courthouse lawn. It was shaded by a duo of old cottonwoods. A local funeral home had painted their name in capital letters on the top plank of the back of the bench. On the middle and bottom planks they had stenciled a message extolling the virtues of pre-planning your funeral. My family wouldn't care and I didn't give a damn.

I sat down on the bench in the shade to wait for Hank. I leaned my sweaty back against Rollerman's message and smiled to myself. The coffee was strong and hot against my tongue. It reminded me of the man across the street. I couldn't blame him for being bitter and tired. Fifty years of memories was sure to be quite a burden. Perhaps he was wise to lay them down while there was still time, before they broke him completely down, even if it ripped at his heart. There might be another chance for him. I knew we both doubted it though.

CHAPTER 27

Twenty-five minutes later people began to trickle down the courthouse steps. A thin lady in a canary yellow sundress, an old man in a light gray suit complete with bent back and ivory handled cane, two teenage boys with cigarettes dangling from their fingers and nerves jumping in their faces, a fat man in a lime green jacket that hadn't seen a dry cleaner's establishment in months. Quite a crew. I watched them walk on by, in and out of my world in one hundred and twenty seconds flat. I wanted another cup of coffee.

Hank walked down the steps with a short, dark-haired woman in a severely cut blue suit. She was doing a lot of talking. I could see her lips move and faintly hear her waspish buzz. Hank was doing a lot of listening. At least he wasn't talking. His eyes were staring straight ahead. I had seen that look a hundred times before. He wasn't seeing anything the rest of us were. The past was alive once again.

They paused as they came to the bench. The woman was still talking. "So you'll call Albuquerque on the Klingman case."

"First thing in the morning. Donaldson is in court this afternoon."

"What about Gilcrist?"

"He's doing sixty days in the Barstow jail. Just started a week ago tomorrow. He'll keep." Hank couldn't quite hide the boredom in his voice.

I was watching her thin, pinched face and saw her pick up on it. Her mouth opened quickly, but she shut it and closed her eyes for a second. When she opened them the fires were banked. "Keep me informed, Sergeant."

"Okay."

"And first, not after the mayor and half the city council."

Hank's eyes were stones set in a granite sculpture. "I said I'd call you.'

Her eyes ran swiftly over his face. She would know him at midnight during the dark of the moon. Without speaking, she spun on her heel and marched, double-time, back the way she had come. It was only after she was gone that I realized that she could have been pretty if she had tried.

CHAPTER 28

I pushed myself up off the bench, and walked gingerly toward Hank. Stiff from too much sitting, my legs ached like they belonged on an eighty year old man, rather than a guy on the dark side of thirty.

Hank caught my approach out of the corner of his eyes. Turning his head in my direction he gave me the evil eye. "You move like an old man, Ward Evans."

"I've had a hard life."

"You are a hard life, although I'm not sure that is quite the same."

"It's not. Had lunch?"

"No, but I'm ready." He consulted his Timex. "My shift officially ended eleven minutes and forty-five seconds ago."

Hank ran the palm of his big left hand back and forth across the back of his neck.

"Come on, then. I'll buy." I started down the sidewalk in the direction of a little diner I knew.

Suddenly a heavy weight thumped down on my left shoulder. I glanced over that way. It was Hank's big right hand. The hair grew as thick and dark as animal fur on the back, running all the way to the first joint of his fingers.

"Whoa, not so fast, Mr. Big Bucks. I know a special little place where you can spend some of your ill-gotten gain. About time one of you high-flying private swingers did a little something for a poor, underpaid public servant. After all, we do the real work."

I swallowed the caustic retort that had formed at the tip of my tongue. There was enough truth in his words to give the benefit of the doubt to a man the size of Hank. We turned together and started walking west. Our early afternoon shadows floated before us.

*   *   *

Hank's special place turned out to be a Mexican joint in an alleyway between San Raphael and Dunelt. It didn't have a name that I could see. Hank told me that the specialties were tacos and tequila. As we fought our way past the buzzing flies and strange odors, I would have figured on Montezuma's revenge as a featured item.

A heavy set woman, whose dark hair hung down in her face and shielded her eyes, escorted us to our booth and took our order. We both passed on the tacos.

The booths were done in imitation leather, but the tequila was the real thing. It burned and bit, and settled at the pit of my empty stomach like a boulder straying from an avalanche. I gasped for air and dabbed at my eyes with a paper napkin.

When I could speak I asked Hank, "How did you stumble across this jewel of the desert?"

He knocked back the rest of his tequila and grinned. "It was last February, early March, and a couple of illegal visitors from old Mexico had a genuine disagreement over a certain señorita. Well, to give you the Reader's Digest condensed version, words led to blows, and blows to knives, and knives to blood. Blood was where I came in.

"Guess I handed the situation in a manner that pleased management, because after the ambulance and the rest of the boys in the band had left, they treated me to a bottle of the best and all the tacos my stomach could handle. Been coming here every week or so since."

"To eat, or drink?"

Hank snorted. "Both." Then he looked at me down the side of his Roman nose. "Maybe a little more drinking than eating. Although you could never tell it from my waistline."

I let me eyes travel over the crags and crevices of his face. "Thought you had given it up."

"I did, for a while. But then—"

"Then what."

He shrugged. "You know, the memories. They don't ever really go away. Just hide for a little while. Then, when you are all unsuspecting, they slide in through the back door. Alcohol helps keep the door shut a little longer."

For a second his eyes found mine. Then they flicked away and he lifted his glass to his lips. It looked like doll china in his huge fist. The remaining contents of the glass slid down his throat like water.

*   *   *

We were two shots beyond the pale, at least I was. As the night wore down and the tequila flowed, Hank grew more silent, while I became downright loquacious.

"You think, Hank, that maybe it's a case of too much time alone?"

123

"What's that?"

"The way I feel about her."

Hank tilted his shot glass back until the liquid ceased flowing. Then he ran loops with his thick pink tongue around the inside of the glass. Finally he placed the glass back precisely on the damp ring on the table and eyed me solemnly.

"What her?"

"The girl I was telling you about. The one who came down the hill to my adobe. The one I bumped into at the old house at the edge of the reservation."

"What about her?"

I shrugged and peered into my glass. There were no answers floating on top of the tequila.

"Why is she on my mind?"

"Is she really there?"

"Yes, she's there. I can sense her always standing just beyond the conscious, waiting on something to appear."

Hank waggled two sausages masquerading as fingers at the waitress. She smiled at him like it hurt.

"I thought you said you had seen her."

"I have."

"Then what do you mean appear."

I sipped at my tequila and considered the question. "I guess I mean right now she is just some nebulous creature creeping around the dark corners of my mind. Only every now and then she shows herself for a moment, and then I am just more confused than ever."

"Confused about what?"

"What she's doing in my life. Especially right now."

Hank leaned forward until his cannonball head intruded deeply into my space.

"What do you mean right now?"

"Why's she here in my life, now, right now? Why has she chosen this particular moment to drift into my private world?"

"You special, boy? You own the whole world?"

"Maybe just a little piece of it. My own private purple adobe."

"Are you going New Age on me, boy?"

"No, man. Just getting drunk."

"It won't help," he said with conviction.

The waitress arrived and waited until Hank had paid for the drinks and over-tipped her. She gently rubbed the back of his neck with long, supple fingers. None of them were encumbered with a ring. She treated him like a favorite, generous uncle. He treated her with genuine affection, yet without sexual overtones.

When she twisted away, I picked up the dangling thread of our conversation. "What do you mean it doesn't help."

A puzzled look spread across Hanks' leather face like warm, low-fat mayo. "Evans, what in the hell are you talking about?"

I took a sip of my tequila. It tasted as old as the night felt. "You said alcohol doesn't help."

Recognition slowly burned away the haze that had clouded his eyes. "Yeah, Ward, that's right. Drinking don't help, not really. Oh, for a few hours maybe, it dulls the ache. But then you wake up and all the agony is right back in your brain. Plus you have the headache from hell."

"Sounds like you've been there."

"More times than I care to remember, son."

I knew the answer, but I asked anyway. "You still miss him, don't you?"

"Every fucking day, you bastard."

Seeing a grown man cry is beyond pain. I couldn't stand it. I pushed my chair back, got to my feet without knowing how, and stumbled unseeing across the floor. I slid my hands along the concrete block wall until I found the men's room. Then I puked my guts out.

CHAPTER 29

About midnight I poured us both into the back seat of a cab. I was damn near broke and sure as hell drunk. I wasn't sure of Hank's financial condition, but he was a very long way from sobriety. In fact, he was so far gone that he had acquired a certain stiffness as if the alcohol had contained a preserving agent. Getting his body into the back seat was much like trying to stuff a six foot, four inch piece of plywood through the narrow opening created by the back door. With the cab driver's help I made it. By the time I had maneuvered myself onto the cloth seat next to him even his face had achieved a certain rigidity. This lent him an aura of nobility. As the cab rolled on through the night, in the half-light of the street lamps, he looked for all the world like an Aztec priest, frozen by the power of the centuries.

I made the driver stop twice on the way to Hank's apartment. The first time on Mineola Street to let me puke on some stranger's front lawn. The second time at an all-night café, I think it was called Jolene's, or maybe that was the name on the tag of the waitress who poured me an oily black coffee in a large white Styrofoam cup, to go. I gave her two dollars and she gave me her best after-midnight smile. She was missing a molar on the left side of her mouth.

Between the vomiting and the caffeine I was sobering up rapidly by the time we reached Hank's place. It was somewhere way up the hill on Grande. With the assistance of the cab driver, I was able to frog-march Hank up the steps to his place. I fished in his pocket and found his keys and a twenty dollar bill. We took off his shoes and socks, and stretched him out on his Swedish modern sectional. He was snoring gently as we let ourselves out. I needed only a little help in navigating back to the cab.

Sobriety was coming with a rush by the time we got back to the Pueblo de Bandas. My head ached like it was splitting into eighths, my ears rang, and little pinpoints of light flickered before my eyes. I was thinking more clearly with every minute that passed and was able to maneuver under my own power. I gave the cab driver the twenty and my thanks. He said, "*De nada.*" I told him to keep the change.

* * *

Gravel scrunched beneath my feet as I crossed the parking lot to number 14. The wind was kicking up and it picked at my shirt and played with my hair. Half-obscured by clouds, the moon glowed silver in the night sky and strange shadows danced before me on the open ground.

All the cabins were dark. Only a single bulb burned into the storage room behind the offices. Far in the distance a dog howled and the wind rustled the leafy branches of the mesquite trees that grew between the cabins. I tugged the large brass key from my pocket and stuck it into the keyhole. They heavy door swung open under the weight of my body and I stepped inside.

There was the sensing before the knowing, and the knowing before the seeing. I froze with my hand on the light switch with as my eyes adjusted to the nearly total darkness of the room. With great clarity I realized that my body was backlit beautifully by the security lights that bordered the parking lot. The thick darkness of my backlit torso made a wonderful target.

It was the silver hair that I saw first. He must have been wearing dark clothes. He blended in so well with the chair. As my eyes adjusted I could begin to see his face, the skin lighter than the dark chair behind him. Seeing only his head was very strange as if it had somehow become disembodied, floating like an avenging apparition in my room. A stray shaft of moonlight glinted off metal roughly two feet below his head. Sweat began to trickle down the back of my neck. I was stone cold sober.

"You've kept me waiting, Mr. Evans."

"If only you had let me know that you were coming. I'd have been home much earlier."

"Oh, I think surprise visits are so much nicer. Don't you agree?"

"Yeah. They're lovely, fucking lovely."

"Now, now, Mr. Evans. Where have all your fine manners gone?"

"They tend to vanish at the sight of a loaded gun pointed in my direction. I assume that the gun is loaded."

"Yes. You may rest assured that it most certainly is loaded."

"You have no idea how much comfort that thought gives me."

As I chatted away I began to try, one very small step at a time, to ease my way back toward the door. I didn't really expect to make it. However, it was better than the alternative, and the best I could come up with at the moment. "And anyway, why are you, or your henchmen, always pointing a gun at me?"

"Now, now, Mr. Evans. Do stand still while we have our final little chat. Except for the ignorance and ineptitude of my former associates you would already be a dead man. I'm afraid that your brief reprieve is just about to come to an end. But, I digress. To answer your succinct question, I continue to cause guns to be pointed at you because you continue to deprive me of the most precious thing in the world to me, my daughter."

I shook my head and eased one step closer to the door. "Afraid I can't take the credit for that, Miller, or whatever your name really is. You screwed that up all by yourself. Abandonment, drugs, booze and sex, that's quite a list there, especially for such a loving father."

My eyes had begun to adjust, and when the wind blew strongly among the mesquite branches shafts of silver from the security lights filtered into the room. Every now and then a band of light fell across the lower half of his face, highlighting his long thin nose, full-lipped mouth and dimpled chin. He looked rather handsome in a mature, slightly shop-worn manner. Only his eyes were still shrouded in darkness. Unfortunately, his eyes were what I really wanted, needed, to see. There would be a fraction of a second after they changed before the hammer would fall, and that would be all the advance notice I would ever receive.

He smiled at me now, teeth white as bones between his tanned cheeks, casting a supercilious air that made me wonder how much time I really had left.

"You judge me cruelly and unfairly, Mr. Evans. I was only trying to make our reunion special for my daughter. As for abandonment, nothing could be farther from the truth. On the contrary, it was my ex-wife's vicious lies and rumor-mongering that drove me out and decided my fate before the judge in divorce court. In those days the law almost always favored the mother and her lies only sealed my casket. That woman has a vivid imagination and a nasty tongue. I still have the verbal scars."

"And the physical ones." I watched his mouth change as I slid another step closer to freedom.

I could hear the change in the timbre of his voice as he spoke.

"Ah, yes. I have a few of those sort of scars, too. I see you really know my wife, Mr. Evans. If only we had more time we could compare notes. You're more intelligent than I originally surmised and more resourceful. In a different place, a different time, we might join forces." He sighed softly to himself. "But now we must end this little party. It's gone on far too long. The night is no longer young, and, alas, Mr. Evans, neither am I. So move, if you please."

He rose from the chair. The gun never wavered. I was watching so very carefully to be sure. He gestured with the gun toward the door.

"Now, Mr. Evans, we will take a little ride and then it will soon be all over for you. Actually, I would prefer to end it now, but that would be too noisy in a neighborhood such as this. No use borrowing trouble."

He stepped through the darkness and crossed the room. The barrel of the gun was hard against my ribs. "Go now. My car is just around the corner. You'll drive and I'll navigate. Won't that be lovely."

I didn't say a word. I couldn't think of anything to say right then. He was my shadow all the way to the door. The gun never left my side.

As we stepped out into the night the wind was cool against my skin. Then I realized that my clothes were damp with sweat. Fear is an awesome thing.

The gravel crunched beneath our feet as we strolled, inches apart, like two old college chums. A little thought had been bubbling in the depths of my brain. It worked its way to the surface.

"I thought you were supposed to be behind bars, Miller."

He chuckled in my ear. The gun stayed in my ribs. "The American justice system is wonderful. With the right attorney, enough of the wrong money, and a judge with a certain bent almost anything is possible." He chuckled again. "I know these things, old buddy, and I use my brain. That is why I'm out on bail while the rest of them linger in a flea infested jail. Isn't life lovely?"

"Fucking lovely," I said to keep the conversation moving and try to cover all contingencies. We were nearing the end of the gravel. Only a few more steps and we would leave the compound. Then it was a few steps on the sidewalk, followed by a short ride to oblivion. Maybe it was imagination or the wind playing tricks on me with the tree leaves, but, out of the corner of my eye, I thought that a moment ago I had seen a shape or shadow moving quickly across the ground just inside the adobe wall that surrounded the Pueblo de Bandas. If it was just my imagination, my run was almost over. If not, well, even a blind hog finds an acorn now and then.

I tried to slow my pace, but the gun in my ribs urged me on. I mumbled some foolishness about not adding murder to his list of crimes, but Miller was through talking. We were a half dozen steps from the sidewalk and he was anxious for the end. The gun prodded harder against my ribs, doing his talking for him.

In the final strides I made up my mind. As we stepped up to the sidewalk I would do something. Taking a ride made no sense. I didn't intend to make it easy for him and, if things got messy, better here than the wilds of New Mexico.

My heart was pounding so furiously that my chest had begun to ache. My nerves were live electrical currents arcing beneath my skin. The strength had suddenly drained from my legs and I moved like a punch-drunk prize fighter trying to go one more round.

Three more steps. Then two. One. I got one foot on the sidewalk, and felt the pressure of the gun ease as Miller negotiated his step up. In that instant, I pivoted and, with everything I had, lunged for Miller's throat.

The screaming inside my skull drowned out the sound of the gun. Pain burned a wicked path along my side and my legs gave away.

The sidewalk reached up and smacked me, then pulled me to its concrete bosom. My mind told my legs to get up and run, but they wouldn't listen. Through a cavalcade of brilliant, spinning stars I could faintly see Miller looming above me. The gun was huge in his hand. Strange shadows danced on the starboard bow.

"So be it," he growled. "Good-bye, Mr. Evans. Good-bye forever." He angled the gun so that the black hole at the end of the barrel pointed directly between my eyes.

I could see my mother. I could see Melissa. I could see the strange woman-girl who haunted my private adobe. I could see Miller grin. I could see the heavy metal shovel arching through the night. Then I could see only the sweaty gray matter inside my own brain, in the instant before it all faded to ebony oblivion.

* * *

I could smell the frijoles on his breath. His face was very close to mine and he was talking very quickly. A dozen bells were tolling incessantly within the walls of my skull and made it very difficult for me to understand the words. The entire right side of my abdomen was coated with a wet, warm liquid that flowed like a river. I closed my eyes and concentrated on the words.

Finally I recognized the voice. It was Juan. The words came to me slowly now, as from a great distance and strained through porous rock.

"Señor Evans, I am sorry. If only I had been sooner. But I was not sure until you were almost across the parking lot, and then it was too late. I am so sorry."

I tried to speak, but the words only gurgled in my throat. The fiery pain in my side was consuming me and I wondered if I were dying. I was keenly aware that question would soon be answered.

"Don't try to talk, Señor. My wife has called for the ambulance and the police. They will be here soon, very soon."

I could feel his hands busy at my side. My brain seemed awash in blood. The pain was horrific and I wanted to cry. I was too scared to do anything though, except pray. Then it seemed as if, far away, across the city, I could hear the wailing moan of a siren. Then again maybe that was only the voice of death.

If death was coming I wanted to see it, and I opened my eyes. Juan was saying something. I saw his lips move, but I could no longer hear. Then I could no longer see. I could only feel the arms of eternity wrapped around me.

CHAPTER 30

On the third day I awoke. I swam slowly into a sea of white. White light filled my eyes and white noise hummed in my ears.

There was sensing, and knowing through sensing. I felt no pain, no hunger, no thirst. I could not even feel my own fingers move. Whether I was alive or dead was open for debate.

I lay very still, and waited for something to happen. Slowly, almost imperceptibly, I became aware of life revolving around me.

Sounds came first. Faintly, as if from a great distance, and garbled. Totally unintelligible. I couldn't even tell if they were voices or machine noises, or cries from the bowels of hell. It didn't bother me, one way or another. I simply floated in my sea of white and listened.

Gradually the white noise abated. I began to comprehend syllables, then words, then sentences, finally whole conversations. I lay very still and listened. I kept my eyes closed. It was way too early to face the light.

The conversations were primarily medical discussions, about my case, and others, interspersed with chit-chat about long hours, car troubles, spouse troubles, financial difficulties, and the actual sighting, by a nurse in pre-op, of a certain surgeon's prodigious private parts.

Then the words became too much and I quit listening. I drifted in a surreal atmosphere, somewhere between fantasy and reality. I could sense dark waves crashing at my feet. In a moment the tide came in and I slept once more.

*   *   *

The pain was there this time when I awoke. I tried to call out for a nurse but my mouth wasn't working well. I fumbled around the side of my bed and found the call button at the end of a thick cord dangling from the metal bed rails.

After a couple of eons, she came. She was young and blonde and pert, and determined to humor me.

She helped me sip a little lukewarm water through a flexible, plastic straw. Lubricated, I asked for some pain medication, my doctor, and a telephone. She gave me a pill to ease the pain, told me she would let the doctor know I was alert, and ignored the issue of the telephone.

She was wise to avoid dealing with the phone. I wasn't ready to talk to anyone. I wasn't even sure who I wanted to call. On the other hand, she was way off-base about alert. Maybe I was a better actor than I gave myself credit for. In less than five minutes I felt consciousness slipping away down a long, dark tunnel. I opened my arms and closed my eyes.

*   *   *

I was sitting up and taking nourishment when Nichols lumbered into my room. He had his head down, reading from his flip-top black notebook. As he entered the small room the change in lighting caught his attention and he looked up. He seemed surprised to find himself in the middle of a hospital room, especially mine.

"Hey, man. You're sitting up."

"Have been for a couple of days."

"I didn't know, or I'd have been here sooner. The way I heard it you were damn near dead. Instead you're eating, watching TV, having a hell of a good time. For all I know you've been up chasing the nurses."

"That's more your line. Anyway, I am going to live. Actually, the bullet just nicked a vein or artery or some such and I lost a lot of blood, but no major damage. If I show good progress, behave myself, and keep their exquisite beef bouillon down they plan to let me out of here this weekend."

I looked at Hank. His face was colored with fatigue and worry. It wasn't hard to figure out where the problem lie. "Another tough case?"

He made a face. "More nasty than tough."

"You look tired. Have a seat." I pointed at a cracked green vinyl chair lounging in the corner with my spoon. Bouillon dripped on my sheets. The dark drops looked like bloodstains.

"Thanks." Hank closed his notebook, eased his bulk onto the chair. It creaked in protest.

"Murder?"

"What?" For a moment Hank's face was coated with puzzlement. Then it cleared. "Oh, my case. Yeah, some little gas station attendant got high Monday night and proceeds to field-dress his wife, and her three months pregnant. Damn near flayed her alive before some guy out for a midnight stroll hears the screams and dials 9-1-1 on his mobile. By the time we get there she is long gone and Mr. Deep-fried has started in on himself with a razor blade. Cut off his weasel and three fingers before we could stop him. He's finally come down from cloud nine and I've got to testify at the arraignment in the morning."

"Bad mix."

"Angel dust. Anything can happen with that shit. It hits everybody a little different. You pays your money and you takes your chances."

"I don't like those odds."

Hank nodded. "Me neither. Sooner or later you're going to lose. The only question is when."

We stared at the walls and each other for a few minutes. I took a sip of my broth. It had gone too cool to eat. That was no loss. Hank restlessly shifted his bulk. The chair groaned again.

"Hey, listen. I didn't come here to talk shop. I came here to see you. You really doing okay, or was all that early release crap for my benefit?"

I smiled to demonstrate my sincerity. "No. That was truth. I'm cool. Just need to get some strength back."

"I should have known. Only the good die young, and you ain't been good for twenty years." He grinned at me, making him look like a bear, in a three-piece suit, with indigestion. "Least that's the story I heard." He sighed and picked himself out of his chair. This time they both groaned. Growing old is hell.

He crossed the polished linoleum, moving lightly and with a grace surprising for a bear, or an old police sergeant. He squeezed my bicep. It was like being trapped in a vice-grip. "You need anything."

"No, I'm just fine. The nurses take good care of me. If I didn't know better I would think that they wanted me to go home soon."

Hank grinned again. This time he looked sad. There again, maybe he really had indigestion. "Well, hate to run Ward, but I'd better go. Got to interview a witness to a drive-by, and he lives way the hell over on Hadley Court." He turned to go. "You take care," he said over his shoulder. "And dodge the next bullet."

"Hank."

He stopped and turned his big ugly head. "Yeah."

"Melissa, how's she doing?"

"Making progress, I guess." Disgust rippled across his face. "Anyway, that's what the pricky little doctor says. He still won't let me see her. Says she needs time to forget. And with time there's hope."

"There's always hope, Hank."

"Yeah. Hope springs eternal, they say. Or some such crap."

"At least you've got Miller for sure now."

"Yeah, as soon as he gets out of the hospital. But you didn't know he was here, did you?"

"I had no idea."

"Yeah, one floor below, with a head split half open by a shovel. You owe somebody a big thanks."

"I know. I'll stop by on my way out of town."

Hank looked at me, but I couldn't read the message in his eyes. "Ward, take care of yourself. Your luck is going to run out." His upper lip twitched. Maybe you better get yourself a woman."

"Maybe I've got one."

"No shit."

"I'll find out when I get back home."

"Anybody I know?" He raised his eyebrows in punctuation.

"I don't think so. I don't really know her myself."

An awkward silence rose between us. Hank broke it. "Good luck, you'll need it. Don't be a stranger."

"I won't. You come see me. I gave you the directions last year."

"Okay, but I've got to scoot."

We were both lying. We both knew it. He was halfway out the door before I stopped him. "Hank."

"Yeah." He answered without turning around.

"You making it?"

"Yeah, sure. One day at a time. One fucking day at a time." Then he raised a hand and walked away. He never looked back. I watched him until all I could see was his shadow sliding down the wall. Then it disappeared into a world beyond my vision. Only the memories lingered.

*   *   *

By Friday night I was pacing the hallways. Two pints of A-negative and a few days of R and R and I was ready to get the hell out of Santa Fe. I love of lot of things about the town, but Melissa was in good hands finally and I was too long gone from my own adobe. Hank knew where to find me when it came time for me to testify. They finally sprung me Saturday morning.

A young patrolman named Gleebeck had come by on Thursday and told me where to find my vehicle. I crossed the sun-baked asphalt on shaky legs. The morning sun was strong, intense, and undiluted. I was soaked with sweat and trembling by the time I pulled myself in behind the wheel.

I took a detour on my way out of town. Juan was repainting the front of the office screen door as I rolled into the parking lot. He was covering the eggshell white with turquoise. As my tires crunched the last ten yards of gravel he looked up, recognized me, and smiled widely.

He laid the brush across the top of the paint can and ambled over to my side of the Cherokee. "Señor Evans, so good to see you up and about."

"It's good to be alive. I owe you a hell of a debt, Juan."

He shook his head vigorously. "No. No. You owe me nothing, amigo. That man, he was going to kill you, a customer, a nice person, on my property."

"Juan, you saved my life."

"*De nada.*"

I looked into his large, brown eyes for a long time. They were dark and deeper than I could probe. Finally, I simply stuck out my hand. He shook it. His calluses were rough against my palm.

"I'd better roll."

Juan nodded. "You are okay to drive all that way by yourself?"

"Yeah. They filled me up with two pints of blood and a gallon of bullion at the hospital. I'm good for another thirty-five hundred miles."

A wide grin threatened to split Juan's face in two. "I have given blood at the hospital many times."

"What type blood?"

"A-negative."

"That's my favorite."

The grin softened to a gentle smile that worked its way north to his eyes. "I know. I asked. You were surely going to need blood and they often run low of our type."

"Maybe I've got some of your blood, Juan."

"Perhaps so, señor."

"That would make us sort of kin."

Juan nodded his head. His black hair shone like polished obsidian in the light of the desert sun. "We are all brothers, amigo."

There was noting much more to say. I flipped him a salute and shifted into reverse. I looked back once in the rearview mirror. Juan was still standing in the gravel, shading his eyes with a flattened hand, following my progress. His little boy joined him. The little fellow had one arm around one of his daddy's legs. With the other hand he was shading his eyes, just like his old man.

CHAPTER 31

She came at dusk, at dusk of the third day. She came to me at dusk of the third day.

I was sitting at my table, the oak smooth as glass beneath my palms. My second post-supper cup of coffee sat steaming before me, as hot as the day had been before the dusk. The dishes were stacked in the drainer behind me, and the evening stretched before like a long, lonely stretch of faintly familiar road.

The sun had fallen behind the mesa tops and the long shadows of evening stretched their dark fingers to meet the purple twilight. The blast furnace heat of the day had vanished leaving behind a decidedly warm afterglow. I was wearing only a ragged pair of Levi cutoffs and last year's running shoes. Often at this time of day a pair of coyotes emerged from the shadows and padded silently over the hill. I was watching for them when she stepped out of the shadows.

She stood so still, unsmiling and unblinking, for so long that I began to think she was only a mirage. Then she suddenly cocked her head to one side like a bird. She listened, or seemed to, for at least two minutes. Satisfied at last, she looked once over her shoulders and began walking slowly across the sand and stones toward the soft, silent shadows of my adobe.

About ten yards from the adobe, deep in the spreading shadows that foretold the coming of night, she saw me. The door was open and I could see her face, but the darkness hid her features and rendered her expression unreadable. I felt naked and exposed in the light from the twin lanterns that sat on the wide adobe windowsill. I knew she could see me as well as if it were daylight, and I struggled to keep all emotion from my face. I counted to five as slowly as I knew how. Then I raised my right arm and motioned for her to come inside.

Thirty seconds passed as if they were eons. Fifteen more were an eternity. I felt like a complete fool, but I could feel my heart beating faster. A nerve pounded at my temples and a lump rose thick and heavy, like a block of coal, in my throat. I forced myself to breathe deeply three times, and to show how cool and unaffected by my visitor I was, I picked up my coffee cup and pulled it to my lips. Then a tremor ran through my hands like quicksilver and I was betrayed. I spoke to hide my embarrassment.

"Welcome to the Hotel California."

"You are very silly, old man." Her voice was light on the air and pitched lower than I expected.

"Sometimes I am."

She turned her back to me and walked slowly around the modest room. Her eyes roamed over the smooth adobe walls, adorned as they were with my meager possessions. She picked up my Caesars mug that I bought on my last trip to Vegas five years ago.

"Want some coffee?"

It was my favorite coffee cup and a thousand wonders that I hadn't broken it already. A year or so ago in a perverse fit of self-imposed discipline I had put it up for future use by my visitors. Except for Gloria Gibson, I hadn't had any.

A slender brown finger ran along an empty mantel shelf above the stone fireplace. I knew it left a path in the accumulated dust. She held the cup in one hand and eyed it cautiously. Her thick black eyebrows formed twin arches as she examined it.

"So you found the girl."

I knew better than to ask, what girl. The grapevine of the sand and sagebrush was a potent one. Gloria had probably had to stop once or twice to get directions. That would have been enough. There weren't many women like Gloria Gibson, certainly not in these parts. I nodded in silent assent. She didn't own me.

She turned to face me, and her wide mouth parted in a parody of a smile. "So now you are the big heroic private investigator." Her words were highlighted with the faint blush of an accent, an accent I could not name.

Her questions were essentially judgments; judgments with which I was not comfortable. A thin line of sweat began to bead across my forehead. I countered with a most basic of conversational gambits. "What's your name?"

Mahogany eyes stared at me for a moment as though I were some bizarre, grotesque species of Gila monster. Then she blinked and they were again twin fires burning dully in a bronze face. Her teeth were white and straight.

"Page."

"As in a book?"

"As in a small town near Lake Powell."

She turned abruptly and walked around the Santa Fe wall that separated my bedroom from the other room that made up my house. The bedroom was small, dark, and held only a single bed pushed up against the wall, an ancient walnut chest of drawers that had been my mother's, and a rickety nightstand that I had bought for five dollars at a flea market in Flagstaff. My last picture of Karen stood in the plastic Wal-Mart frame on top of the dust. Page didn't stay thirty seconds.

"Is the girl all right?"

"She's better off now than she was."

"You don't sound happy."

"You're very insightful. Especially for one so young."

She smiled as if she possessed a precious Christmas secret. "I am many things. Including being twenty-one." A certain bright light danced deep in the depths of her mahogany eyes.

I took another drink of my coffee. It was barely lukewarm. "Want to name some of them?"

She only smiled.

The darkness had fallen across the desert like a Navajo blanket. The light from my lamps spilled flickering pools of amber across sand and shadow. An animal rustled through the yard. Too dark to see, it sounded small and insignificant. I understood that perception. A thousand questions jostled for prominence in my mind. I asked one that didn't matter.

"Want something to eat?"

"No, thanks."

She came over slowly to the table and sat down in my dusty spare chair. I could feel neurological impulses traveling up and down my body. They were wild and free and moved with self-will. It was very strange having someone else sitting at my table. My adobe had been my private desert castle keep for a long time. I felt strangely violated, even if Page didn't look particularly like the Black Knight.

"You live at Ridgeview?"

"Just a mile on the other side."

"I remember you from the abandoned house."

She lay her hands on my table, palms down. They were nice hands. They looked strong and competent. She wore no rings. There was no watch on either of her wrists. A small scar, roughly the shape of the Baja Peninsula, ran north to south between the thumb and forefinger of her left hand.

"I remember you too from there, and other places."

"What other places?"

She smiled. "Many other places and times. Most of them you will have forgotten by now, but I remember. I will always remember."

The girl spooked me. She spoke in riddles and mysteries. Yet there was truth in her words. Undeniable truth. Even I could hear it. I smiled back to camouflage my fears.

"Do you go to the old house often?"

She shrugged. Her shoulders moved smoothly inside the oversized men's white dress shirt that she wore tucked into well-worn Levis. "When I want to be alone."

"Big family?"

"Two brothers, two step-brothers, a sister and a step-sister." I couldn't tell whether she was happy or not with her siblings.

"So I fouled you up by being there that day."

She turned her hands over and examined her palms. Page's eyes slowly came up to meet mine. "Well, I wasn't planning on you."

"Being there, you mean?"

Her pink tongue licked her lips. Her brown eyes were as ancient as the sun. "Period."

Silence grew slowly between us. Time had decided to stand still in the desert that evening. After five minutes, the silence began to spread through me like a madness. I found that profoundly strange since I often spent days, even weeks, in a self-imposed cocoon of silence. The difference was not in the night, nor in me, but in the presence of the strange woman who disturbed the serenity of my self-imposed exile.

After ten minutes, my own impatience was too much for me to bear and I pushed my chair away from the table. Page's eyes were on my face, but they were not seeing me. I couldn't tell what they were seeing. I got up and walked to the open door and slipped outside. Page never moved a muscle.

A wild animal scurried furtively in the small stand of sagebrush that grew in the shadows of the triangular rocky ledge that broke the symmetry of the hillside as it jutted skyward only yards east of my doorway. A waning moon had risen, creamy in the vast indigo sky, and silvery light spilled from the surface like albino blood from a gunshot elk. It lit the path that ran from my shadow down to the canyon floor. It was strangely brilliant, so nearly like the beginning of the day that it was difficult to tell the difference. I followed the moonlight until the adobe was only a murky image against the intestinal black bowels of the hillside.

A stout breeze had sprung up with the dark, and its cool fingers filtered through the scraggly mesquite and traced unknown patterns on my weathered cheeks and the back of my neck. A bird, whose call I could not name, whistled, cajoling its mate in the gathering darkness. Deep on the rim of the western sky, just at the precipice of the far horizon, a hint of gold persisted. Below me the canyon floor was huge, and black as death.

I sat in the stillness that defines the desert as night falls across a sea of sand. There is a sadness in the silence, but also a comfort. Yet, most of all, there is certainty, a certainty as sure as either life or death. I waited in silence and gathering purple darkness as the saguaro cactuses that littered the landscape held a final sacred silent vigil. Together we waited for the embrace of the night.

* * *

It was so dark I could not see the face of my watch held six inches from my face. The moon was old and tired and too bled out to fight through the dark gray clouds that were blowing in from the west, thickening on the horizon. They blotted out the stars with the promise of rain. Clouds were like most of the women I had known in my life, long on promise and short on delivery. William Shakespeare said it best, as he so often did: "Full of sound and fury, signifying nothing."

I sensed her presence long before I could verify she was there. Maybe it was the ancestral memories, imbedded deep into the core of my brain, that triggered the acuteness of the senses that set my nerves on edge. Perhaps it was just the stray scent of her own body odor that wafted on the wind. I couldn't say for certain, not that it really mattered. She was just there, suddenly and silently, three feet and a million light years away. I sat still and held my own counsel; an out-of-work private eye, on the dark side of thirty, alone and scared in the dark emptiness of the world.

She was closer now. I could hear her soft breathing. I could not see her though, and I was afraid. Afraid of her, and more, more even than I would admit to myself. I longed for the light of the moon or a dozen dying stars and I silently prayed to the angels of the night. But, like a jilted lover, they answered me not. I felt the brush of her hair against my bare biceps, the smoothness of her palm caressing my cheek.

Her lips were as soft against my cracked dry ones as the first petal of the first flower of spring. Gently searching at first, they were soon hungrily roving across my mouth. I felt the tip of her tongue lick quickly against the inside of my mouth as she pulled me to her. I fumbled with the buttons on her shirt and the world began to whirl around the distant stars. Flesh melted against flesh, and we were separate no more. As though from a great distance I heard her moan softly to herself and my own cry sounded sharp and strange in my ears.

Then, a great rushing silence filled my mind, and the world was young once more.

CHAPTER 32

I lay on my side, my head propped up on one hand, and watched daylight drift slowly in through the green window, its golden light gradually gaining. The last purple vestiges of the evening shadows soon became only a few purple visions crouched warily in the four adobe corners and under our bed.

Page was warm and smooth as old daylight as she curled against me. Her breath came smooth and slow and sweet. Her long eyelashes fluttered from time to time, but she didn't awaken. Her hair spilled darkly across the pillow, and one slim arm dangled over the side of the captain's bed we shared.

Naked beneath the sheets she was amazingly soft for someone who looked so young and thin. Faded blue jeans and oversized men's flannel shirts had cleverly disguised her passage to womanhood. I let my right hand slowly transverse the swell of her hip.

A dove cooed softly in the scrub and mesquite that grew just east of the adobe, and in a few seconds another answered. The morning breeze played with the curtain at the window. Its force was just strong enough to caress my face. The stubble on my cheek was ten days old. There were thousands of miles on my scarred, battered legs, and more lines in my face than a road map of east L.A., but I felt as young as tomorrow morning.

God, Son, or the Holy Ghost had flung a handful of freckles across her cheeks. They staggered across her face like the last remnants of Lee's army on the road to Appomattox. I followed their line of march up her cheekbones and across the ridge of her nose, then I lowered my head and gently kissed her eyelids. She snuggled more deeply against me. I lay as still and silent as the purple adobe wall behind me and watched golden life spill into the room.

THE END

ABOUT THE AUTHOR

Christopher James Helvey, one of Kentucky's hottest new writers, debuts on the national scene with his action packed, emotionally supercharged, insightful first novel, *Purple Adobe.* His short stories and poetry are already familiar to readers across the South, having appeared in numerous publications including *Kentucky Monthly, Kudzu, Iodiolect, Kentucky Blue, Beginnings* 99, and *Ace Weekly.* He has been a featured reader of his short stories at the Carnegie Center in Lexington, and a presenter at the Frankfort Arts Showcase. He lives with his family in Kentucky's capital city where he is working on his next novel.

Printed in the United States
20375LVS00005B/407

9 780759 698765